I0745644

# COPPER

## Mage

## OTHER BOOKS BY DOROTHY DREYER

Phoenix Descending

Paragon Rising

Cauldron of Ash

Christmas in Silverwood

## THE EMPIRE OF THE LOTUS SERIES

Crimson Mage

Copper Mage

Golden Mage

Emerald Mage

Sapphire Mage

Amethyst Mage

Diamond Mage

# COPPER

## *Mage*

EMPIRE OF THE LOTUS

BOOK TWO

DOROTHY DREYER

**Copper Mage**
**Empire of the Lotus Book Two**
Second Edition

Copyright © 2019 Dorothy Dreyer
Edited by Amy McNulty
Cover design by Sora Sanders

ISBN: 978-1-948661-42-3

Published March 2020 by Snowy Wings Publishing
PO Box 1035, Turner, OR 97392

This is a work of fiction. Names, characters, places, and incidents either are the product of the author's imagination or are used fictitiously. Any resemblance to actual persons, living or dead, or locales is entirely coincidental.

All rights reserved. No part of this publication may be reproduced, distributed, or transmitted in any form or by any means, including photocopying, recording, or other electronic or mechanical methods, without the prior written permission of the publisher, except in the case of brief quotations embodied in critical reviews and certain other noncommercial uses permitted by copyright law.

*For those who stuck by me
during my ups as well as my downs*

Arcane daggers. Mysterious Scrolls. A vengeful dark god determined to end the world.

The soldiers of the shadow army are on the rise. The ancient deity Kashmeru has the Lotus empress under his control. It's up to the elite mages of the Empire of the Lotus to put an end to the dark god's course of death and destruction.

But mage powers have been outlawed, and not all mages are free. As Mayhara evades the Imperial Police on her quest to gather the elite mages, Shiro must do what is necessary to escape the prison camp he's been trapped in for years.

The collapse of the universe is at hand, and the pieces of the puzzle must be put together before it's too late.

*An intense copper calm, like a universal yellow lotus, was more and more unfolding its noiseless measureless leaves upon the sea.*

— Herman Melville

*The legend goes …*

*The ancient deity Kashmeru knew only one true love—the Lotus empress Lakshmi, who in his eyes possessed all beauty and grace the universe could hold. Their hearts called to one another, a hold so strong that neither one could deny the bond. But Lakshmi knew that Kashmeru's spirit was not pure, for an evil dwelled within his soul, a wickedness so corrupt that it could destroy the universe.*

*And when she denied him her love, destroying the universe was the very thing he vowed to do.*

*Throughout the centuries, their reincarnations were drawn to one another, but the outcome was always the same: Lakshmi would never give Kashmeru her heart.*

*To put an end to his constant chase, the Empire of the Lotus defeated Kashmeru and sealed him in a tomb using mage powers, where he would remain trapped …*

*… until the Council of the Seven could secure the blood of the Lotus empress to set him free.*

# THE SEVEN HOUSES OF MAGES

*Crimson*: earth, stability, survival, security.

*Copper*: water, ice, pleasure, guilt.

*Golden*: fire, willpower, shame.

*Emerald*: air, wind, heart, love, grief.

*Sapphire*: throat, sound, truth, lies.

*Amethyst*: vision, sight, illusions, secrets.

*Diamond*: spirituality, emotion, virtue, integrity.

# One

Mayhara cringed as she pulled the computer tower from the rubble, her fingers aching from the bite of the jagged pieces of stone. She couldn't use her powers on the stone; the academy building had been enchanted to withstand mage powers so the students wouldn't accidentally destroy it. Even the bricks that made up the building were unable to be penetrated by the magic. But the enchantment had done nothing against the bullets and battering rams the New Asian Administration had used to destroy the school during the Eradication.

With one final yank, she loosened the machine from where it was wedged, but dread overcame her as she took in the damage the casing had endured. She could only hope the hard drive was still intact. They were relying on the information it contained. She was quick to unscrew the casing and disconnect the hard drive. It was crushed in one corner, but she had to think positive—it would work; it would be fine.

With the hard drive in hand, Mayhara stood. Sirens in the distance caused her to freeze in place. She shouldn't be here. She shouldn't be anywhere, actually, except in a prison camp with her family—which was exactly where she'd end up if she was caught sneaking around the demolished mage academy. Instinctively, she backed up against the wall, her long dark hair falling across her face as she ducked her head.

She waited until the sirens faded, her breaths slowing in relief once they'd passed. Wincing, she realized she'd been crushing the hard drive into her chest. Her grip had been too tight, and a drop of blood bloomed against her deep brown complexion. She adjusted the hardware and steeled her feelings. The fear of getting caught was not only an issue of getting thrown into a prison camp; if she was captured now, her mission would be jeopardized. And if that happened, it could mean the end of the world.

Holding the hard drive securely, she scanned the room. She wasn't sure there would be anything else of use to her in the administration office of the school. She held what she hoped were the complete files of every student who'd ever attended the academy, but she wasn't confident it was all they would need to track down the other elite mages. At least, the ones who had survived.

She shuddered at the thought of the government's war on mages—and worse, the Pishacha's plan to terminate the elites as a direct order from the vengeful deity, Kashmeru. It was bad enough the Lotus empress had slipped from their grasp, unavoidably heeding Kashmeru's call, but Mayhara also had to deal with the fact that an ancient shadow army was out to kill her.

Deciding the hard drive would be enough, she made her way through the fallen bricks and concrete dust and into the hallway. The setting sun barely offered enough light for her to check if her path was clear. She considered using her mage powers to shine some crimson light but thought better of it. She'd just have to travel carefully.

She made it to the end of the hall and approached the stairway leading down to the main floor. Only a third of the stairs was intact, and she had to use some skillful maneuvering to make her way down. Luckily, her tight jacket and fitted, black jeans made tackling the obstacle a little easier. Once she reached the main floor, her eyes immediately went to the damaged hanging tapestry embroidered with the faces of the past Lotus empresses. Centuries of reincarnations of the deity Lakshmi were displayed along the high walls of the great hall, now partially burnt and torn, destroyed in the crossfire during the Eradication.

The only face missing was Naree's.

That was because her family had kept her hidden for years. No one knew she was the reincarnated Lotus empress aside from her family and Darshana, the empire's finest guru. The New Asian Administration didn't know—or at least they hadn't known. For all Mayhara knew, the administration could have found out. And if Mayhara's suspicions were correct and the administration was under the control of the Pishacha, then the fate of the universe was looking rather bleak.

She walked past the rubble that littered the floor and headed for the library. One of the large, wooden double doors hung partially off its hinges. Inside, desks and bookshelves were strewn about on the mosaic-tiled floor. A gaping hole in the wall let in what little was left of the sunlight, the golden beams shining upon the demolished shelves and shredded books. At the far end of the room, Jae crouched over a metal box on the floor.

"Find anything?" she asked him.

Jae turned his head toward her and dropped whatever was in his hands. "Nothing that helps."

He stood and stretched, rolling out his shoulder. For a moment, Mayhara was transfixed by his lean, muscular form, his confident stance, and the heavy set of his brows as he contemplated the situation. He raked a hand through his dark hair and sighed. When his eyes found her again, she cleared her throat and looked down at the hard drive in her hands. It wasn't the first time she'd found herself staring at him. Spending every day with him over the last few weeks, Mayhara had experienced many moments of a quickened heartbeat if he happened to brush her skin, a tingle in her body when they would share a laugh, and the desire to move closer to him while they worked. But she'd always shaken off the feeling as loneliness, as wanting to be close to someone since her family was imprisoned, or simply being in a situation together that not many others would understand. Besides, she couldn't know how he felt, and as brave as she was fighting off Pishacha, she didn't have the nerve to ask him.

Not that there was any time for that, anyway.

They were on a mission to save Jae's sister, to free the spirit of Lakshmi from the evil grasp of Kashmeru, and to ensure the safety of the universe. She had a family she needed to get out of a prison camp, so she shouldn't have wasted a moment wondering if this guy—this former classmate from the Empire of the Lotus Mage Academy— liked her back. It was trivial.

"I found the hard drive," she said, holding it out. "It looks like it took a blow, but maybe we can salvage what's on it."

He strode toward her and held his hands out. She gave him the hardware and then rested her hands on her hips, focusing on their mission once again.

"No way of telling until we get back to the temple," he said. "But the damage appears minor." He flashed her a smile. "I'm hopeful. Good job."

Mayhara ignored the compliment. "No sign of any scrolls?"

"None like the one Darshana described."

"She said it wouldn't be here. She would have recognized it from her vision if it was a scroll that had been kept at the school."

Jae tapped the hard drive against the palm of his hand. "I know. I figured I'd look anyway, just in—" He stopped, lifting his chin.

He'd heard the crumbling before she had. His sapphire powers at work.

With a gasp, Mayhara threw her hands up into the air past Jae's head. A section of the ceiling fell apart, taking with it a metal light fixture that made a direct drop toward where they stood. Quick to use her mage powers, Mayhara released streams of crimson energy, the particles rushing between Jae and the falling debris. The crimson shield solidified, forming a slanted wall that deflected the debris. Her garnet wristband glowed brightly. She pushed out her power until the wall connected sturdily with the floor. As soon as her palms were clear from the crimson dust, Mayhara pulled Jae toward her.

Dust flew around their heads, both from the destroyed ceiling and Mayhara's crimson wall. Jae gaped at how close he had been to getting hit, and then he turned back to Mayhara. They were mere inches apart.

"Are you all right?" she asked.

It took him a moment to respond. He swallowed visibly. "Yes. Thanks."

She averted her eyes. "Yeah, of course."

Her hands were still on his arms. She let them drop, then pushed her hair out of her face, taking a step back. Jae's eyes narrowed slightly, but as he opened his mouth to speak, a buzzing interrupted him.

He pulled his Linq out of his pocket but didn't look long at the screen. "It's Darshana."

"Has she found something out?"

"She didn't say. She just wants us to get back as soon as we can."

Mayhara nodded once. "Then let's go."

# Two

Shiro raced after Qiang, his head kept low and his footsteps light. The heat and the stench made the air thick and difficult to move through. But that was the least of Shiro's concerns. With Qiang leading the way, Shiro and the rest of their gang were determined to make it to the eastern guard station unnoticed. It was only a matter of time before the Imperial Police discovered that the guards patrolling Shiro's camp were missing—and surely soon after they would find them tied up and stuffed in the outhouses, having been knocked out by a couple of Qiang's men. Ten minutes had passed since then, and every second flooded Shiro's heart with panic.

Shiro glanced over his shoulder at the rows and rows of bunkers at the edge of the camp. High above the camp, in the midnight-blue sky, the hazy streak of the Akutake comet marked its place as it made its approach. Seeing the encampment from this distance hit him hard. Long gone were the grassy areas surrounding the bunkers, now trodden down by the heavy boots of the Imperial Police, beaten into mud by the unforgiving monsoons. The cabins themselves appeared as if they were dying, the cracking stone greyed with time, infested with withered vines, the doors and windows falling off their hinges. The outhouses were long forgotten by the Imperial Police, who did nothing to keep them usable. Food rations seemed to get smaller by the week. Shiro had already given up believing the administration intended to keep them alive. This was a death camp. If they wanted to survive, there was no other choice but to escape.

"Keep low," Qiang called out. He signaled for a few of the men to rush ahead. Shiro closed the space between them, huddling close to Qiang's back to await further instructions.

The two men Qiang had sent ahead—Peng and Bao—were lean and light on their feet. They traveled fast, but Shiro suspected it was because they were emerald mages and used air energy to their advantage. If it weren't for Peng's reddish hair and hooked nose, he and Bao could be mistaken for brothers, all long legs and arms. Qiang nodded to Mitty, the burly golden mage whose hair was pulled back in a bun, then twisted to look over his shoulder at Shiro. Their eyes locked, and for a split second, Shiro couldn't breathe. Qiang's black hair hung loose on his forehead, and the stubble on his chin drew emphasis to how square his jaw was.

"Ready?" Qiang asked.

Shiro wasn't sure. He couldn't even keep straight in his head what they were doing. But Qiang had said he'd overheard guards talking about an oncoming attack, and they had apparently mentioned Shiro's name specifically. Qiang and the others were doing this for him. He nodded.

They stood but kept their heads low, approaching the patrol route. A short but loud grunt sounded, and the next thing Shiro knew, Mitty rushed forward, pounding a golden glowing fist into the guard whom Peng and Bao had jumped and pinned to the ground. The guard curled into a ball with a moan. Peng and Bao must have thought that was the end of the fight because they released the guard. They only realized it was a mistake when the guard jumped to his feet with a cyber baton in his grasp.

Shiro mumbled a curse. The weapon served as an advantage over mages, able to block and deflect their powers. It evened the playing field.

The guard snarled as he swung the baton in front of him. He didn't stand at his full height, obviously still affected by Mitty's fiery punch. Peng tried his luck and pounced the guard but was caught in the stomach with the baton. An electric sizzling sounded. Peng yelped in pain and fell to the ground.

Qiang sprang to his feet and rushed toward the scuffle. Mitty flexed his muscles, his fists clenched, circling the guard and assessing his possible strategies of attack. The guard swung his baton in Qiang's direction, which erupted an explosion of fear in Shiro. It would kill him to see Qiang hurt. His palms glowing orange, Shiro whipped his hands through the air. He ignored the excruciating pain that tore through him from using his mage powers and concentrated on the ground the guard stood on. A flash of ice suddenly appeared at the guard's feet. In his shock, he attempted to move back, but he slipped on the ice and landed hard on his backside. Qiang took advantage of the guard's weakened position and used his crimson power to move the earth, crimson particles forming around the guard's arms to hold him down. But the guard was quick to swing his cyber baton, the glowing stick shattering the crimson earth around his left arm.

Before the guard could get a good hit in, Qiang jumped on top of him, grabbed him by his head, and slammed it into the ground. Shiro rushed forward but skidded to a stop when Qiang suddenly slipped a serrated hunting knife out of his boot. Shiro remembered it being smuggled in, but he hadn't seen it since then. Until now. He was barely able to protest whatever Qiang had in mind before Qiang grabbed the guard's face, forced his mouth open, and sliced off his tongue.

Shiro turned away, bile rising in his throat. Tears spilled over his lashes. He hadn't wanted it to come to this. Killing repulsed him. He held his throat, begging himself not to vomit.

He turned back to face Qiang, his heart pounding in

his ears. He tried to avoid looking at the guard, but his eyes deceived him. The guard gurgled as he struggled not to choke on his blood.

"Qiang, what have you done?" Shiro's voice shook.

"What? I didn't kill him." Qiang wiped his knife off on the guard's shirt, then stuck it back in his boot. "This way he can't rat us out to anyone. Let's go. We've got to reach the guard station before they find out."

Shiro could only stare after Qiang as he reminded the team of the plan. Inside his chest, Shiro's heart felt as if it had been pulverized, as if the beating had stopped from the horror of what he'd just seen. He knew they would have to go to some extreme measures in order to get out past the guards, but this just seemed unnecessarily cruel. Or had the guards deserved such treatment for all the years the mages had been forced to suffer under their watch?

Peng and Bao ran ahead, while Mitty dragged the whimpering guard into the bushes to hide him. Shiro heard a sizzle, which he imagined was from Mitty using his fire-control powers to cauterize the guard's tongue stump. At least, he hoped that was what it was.

Shiro was astounded at how Mitty never showed that he was experiencing any pain from using his powers.

When they'd been captured during the Eradication, the New Asian Administration had implanted power blockers into the necks of all mages. But the devices served more like shock collars, transmitting currents of painful electricity into the mage's body upon use of their powers, rather than blocking them. Shiro hadn't been able to move for days after trying to use his water-control powers for the first time after the implant. Water and electricity were a bad mix.

A few months after imprisonment, they'd banded together and had all been practicing, training with Qiang's guidance to block out the pain. Shiro could never entirely block it out. And he suspected Peng and Bao couldn't, either, judging by the clenching of their jaws and twitching of their shoulders when they used their powers. But for Shiro, it was worse. When he used too much mage power, he would be punished with tremors of agony accompanied by a stinging nosebleed. It had always felt as if the blood was literally draining from his brain. But he was determined to endure it in order to escape.

And it was then, in those moments stolen away to train the pain away, that Shiro had grown closer to Qiang. It was then that he'd found a reason to get up every morning, a reason to fight to survive, and a reason to get out of the prison camps and be free—together with Qiang.

He'd imagined what their life together could be like, daydreamed about getting a place together, somewhere off the grid where no one could find them. Nothing big or fancy. Just some place they could call their own.

But first, they would need to escape, and that meant using his mage powers. He only needed to use enough power to get them out of the camp. He just hoped it would be as easy as Qiang had said it would be. And he begged to the gods that no one would have to die in the process.

# Three

Naree stirred, stretching with a pout as she woke from her dream. But it wasn't only a dream; it was a memory from a past life. As Lakshmi, she had sneaked out of the palace in the middle of the night to meet her love, Kashmeru. He had stood beneath a willow tree, hidden from view by the low, swaying branches. Hearing her approach, he had turned to face her, and his smile had mesmerized her.

He had held out a hand. "Lakshmi."

"I'm sorry I'm late," she had replied.

"For you, I would wait an eternity."

Her heart filled with warmth from his words, his gaze, and the intense love she could feel emanating from his core. She had taken his hand and let herself be enveloped by him. He lowered his head, his nose pressed into her hair as his hands gently caressed her back.

"Where shall I take you, my love?" he'd asked.

"Anywhere. As long as you're with me."

Naree smiled at the memory, running her hands along the soft fabric of the bed, wishing it was Kashmeru's arms instead. She wanted to lie there all day, reveling in the feeling, reliving the moments of pure, genuine love.

*Lakshmi, we have some things to take care of, my love.*

She let out a sigh and pushed her feet to the side of the bed. As she swung into a sitting position, her long, straight, black hair fell like silk over her shoulders. Though reluctant to do anything but lounge all day, she couldn't resist Kashmeru's call.

A knock came at the door before it opened. Bhutano stepped in, stopping just inside the room. He wore his uniform, which always confused Naree. He was a shadow spirit, possessing a human body and pretending to be the human as he carried out Kashmeru's plan. Looking at him, no one would suspect that this man would be playing a part in the demise of the universe.

She'd only met him after Bruno disappeared. Before that, Bhutano was the invisible commander, instructing Bruno to protect Naree, to bring her where she needed to be in order to carry out her part of the prophecy. Now that Bruno was gone, Bhutano stepped in to do the job of protector himself.

"Your Highness," he said with a bow.

"Yes, I know," she responded. She stood, grabbing her robe. "I'll get ready."

# Four

Mayhara held tightly to Jae's waist as the motorcycle took a swift curve off the main road and onto a hidden path that led uphill. She wasn't sure if it was the unevenness of the road or her close proximity to Jae that was making her heart jump. As soon as they veered onto the path, the loud roar of the engine cut out. Peering over Jae's shoulder, Mayhara could see a blue glow peeking out from beneath his driving gloves. His sapphire mage powers silenced the engine so they could reach Darshana's hidden temple undetected. The heavy canopy of trees along the path helped as well.

They'd both moved into the temple with the guru shortly after Naree's sudden disappearance following their rescue mission. Darshana had insisted that Naree's knowledge of Jae's apartment was too risky. She could easily divulge his location to the Pishacha, brother or not. Then he'd be a sitting duck. It had taken some convincing, but Jae had finally agreed.

Besides, Bhutano was still out there.

They knew that Bhutano had possessed a human, and they'd assumed it had been Bruno. But after Bruno had lost the fight they had and disappeared into a cloud of black smoke, Jae had intercepted a message that Bhutano was angry that Bruno hadn't shown up at a meeting point. That was when Mayhara and Jae knew Bhutano had been possessing someone else. The problem was they didn't know who.

The temple Darshana had somehow acquired use of—details she mysteriously kept secret—sat quietly, high on the hill, invisible to the road below. Though modest in size for a temple, its pink sandstone columns and white marble tile floors gave it a welcoming, aesthetic beauty. Stone elephants as tall as Jae stood, tusks up, at the entrance, and both inside the temple and out in the gardens, statues of deities could be found—not only Kashmeru and Lakshmi, but also the gods and goddesses of the sun, moon, and sea. Jasmine trees brushed by the hilltop winds blew a calming fragrance through the space. The back of the temple opened up to a floral garden flanked by the hilltop forest. A small, stone, manmade waterfall fed into a clear pond that reflected the stars and the approaching comet at night. Lotus fountains supplied a tranquil sound of gentle, flowing water.

But more importantly, the temple felt safe.

There were more than enough bedrooms for the three of them, and Jae had set up his equipment in the ground-floor office. The laptop that held the files he'd stolen from Bruno was kept open on the office desk, being used daily in an attempt to track down the Pishacha and Naree.

Jae parked his motorcycle in the carport, and Mayhara reluctantly slipped her hands from his waist. Removing her helmet, she shook out her long, dark hair and wiped the beads of sweat from her temples. Jae flashed her a smile as he propped both helmets on the bike. He gave the bike a pat, obviously glad to have it back. After it had been found by the Imperial Police a month ago, Jae had had to abandon it, waiting for the right opportunity to get it back. Mayhara wasn't sure how he had done it, nor had she bothered to ask. She only remembered him leaving the temple one night and returning with it a couple hours later.

Now it looked like it belonged there in the carport, parked between the two used cars that belonged to Darshana. They weren't flashy cars; Darshana had purposely bought boring, ordinary ones they could use to get around without being noticed.

"I wonder what's got Darshana in a huff," Jae said, removing his gloves.

"Could be anything. But she wouldn't have called us back if it weren't something that might help."

He tapped the carrier bag at his side. "Speaking of something that might help, I'm anxious to check if these files are intact."

"Think positive," Mayhara said as they strode toward the entrance. "On both accounts."

Jae glanced at her and halted, gently grabbing her wrist. "Hey."

She blew out a shuddered breath as she stopped alongside him. "What?"

"First of all, unclench your hands."

Mayhara looked down at her white-knuckled fists, only now realizing she was clenching them. She forced herself to relax her hands and then looked up at Jae.

"It won't do us any good if you're wound up so tight." Jae loosely shook her arm, the corner of his mouth inching upward. "Let's just take this one step at a time. It's the most we can do."

"Yeah. Okay. You're right."

He gave her a wink, releasing her arm, then motioned for her to continue with him into the temple.

Out of habit, Mayhara ran her hand along the smooth surface of one of the stone elephants' tusks as they stepped inside.

They didn't have to search for her. They found Darshana in the meditation room, as they'd expected, sitting with her legs crossed, her wrists resting on her knees, and her eyes closed. Her breathing was almost indiscernible. Her long, white hair was pulled into a neat braid that hung down her back. The skilled guru's posture was impeccable; it was almost as if she were a statue. Peace seemed to surround her, like a soft glow that danced upon her being. That, along with her almost wrinkle-free skin, made her look much younger than she actually was.

Jae propped his shoulder against the doorframe and gave Mayhara a sideways smirk. They knew better than to interrupt Darshana when she was meditating. Mayhara caught Jae's expression and bit back a laugh. She knew he must have been thinking about the time they'd been waiting for Darshana to break from her trance, lurking on the sidelines, only for Mayhara to have involuntarily let out a violent sneeze, shocking the guru into losing her balance and falling backward with her legs still crossed in the lotus position in the air.

Jae smiled and shook his head, obviously infected by Mayhara's shaking shoulders as she kept her laughter locked inside.

"That's not helpful," Darshana said flatly, her eyes still closed.

"Sorry, Darshana," Jae and Mayhara replied at the same time.

Darshana placed her palms together and gracefully bowed forward. She then shook out her wrists and opened her eyes. As she got to her feet, she eyed Jae's messenger bag. "Find it?"

"Mayhara did. There's some damage to the casing, but it's probably salvageable." Jae pushed off the door frame. "What did you need us to come back for?"

The old woman moved with poise through the room, blowing out candles. "The vision of the scroll came to me again."

"That's great," Mayhara said.

"I saw more details this time. I thought we should add them to Jae's computer thingy."

"3D simulator," Jae said. "Yeah, let's do it. If this scroll is the key to saving the universe, then we need to figure out what and where it is."

"That's why I called you back," Darshana said. "I thought it best to do it while it's still fresh in my mind. I went back into meditation after I called to see if any other details would appear, but nothing else has come up."

"Okay, well, let's put in what you did see. Who knows? Maybe when you see it on the screen, something else will come to you." Jae stepped aside as Darshana walked past him and toward the office.

Jumbles of wires snaked between Jae's laptop, a couple of external hard drives, and some other equipment

Mayhara couldn't remember the names of. When Jae tapped the laptop's screen, it emanated a blue glow that cast a muted light on the office walls.

"Just pulling up the program," Jae said, his face bathed in blue.

A grid popped up on the monitor, a 3D graphic of a scroll cylinder displayed in the center. Jae placed two fingers on the screen and pulled them in different directions. The scroll rotated.

"The cylinder has a curved design on both ends." Darshana pointed at the screen.

"Okay, let me zoom in," Jae said.

"Curved like the tips of flower petals, linked in a row."

"Like this?"

"No. Pointier."

Mayhara stayed in the doorway to give them room to work as Jae listened to Darshana's description of the scroll and sculpted the details into the graphic in his 3D program. She pulled out her Linq—the new one Jae had gotten for her since her old one was still in the evidence room of the police station—and scanned the news sites for any word of homicides. She knew there was a chance the government could be covering it up, but if any of the media sites let the report of a mage homicide or any other death slip through the cracks of the controlled internet, it could be a lead.

Not only were the elite mages being found murdered all over New United Asia, but seemingly innocent citizens were turning up dead as well. Mayhara had learned that these seemingly innocent victims were actually Sacred Keys, special recruits of the empire, assigned with keeping special daggers safe from the Pishacha. These daggers were connected to the legend they'd all heard as children, one that Mayhara had found out was real.

According to the legend, the ancient deity Kashmeru had known only one true love—the Lotus empress Lakshmi. Lakshmi had been created in pure beauty and grace, a goddess of good. Though Kashmeru's spirit had been filled with evil and corruption, there had remained a connection between them that had withstood centuries. Their hearts had called to one another, time and time again. The hold was so strong, neither one could deny the bond, but Lakshmi denied Kashmeru her love every reincarnation.

She had vowed that she would never give him her heart, and he had vowed to destroy the universe because of this.

To put an end to his constant chase, the Empire of the Lotus had created the mage army, training mages to protect the empress in every reincarnation. They'd defeated Kashmeru and his shadow army of Pishacha and sealed the deity in a tomb. The legend prophesized that he would remain trapped in the tomb unless the Council of the Seven could secure the blood of the Lotus empress to set him free.

Jae's sister, Naree, was the newly reincarnated Lotus empress. And the daggers were the key to get her blood.

Mayhara fought not to hold her breath as she scrolled through the news feed. If she did that, she'd suffocate. She kept an electronic notebook full of names of the deceased mentioned on the sites, placing stars next to the names she recognized. People she'd gone to the academy with—the elite mages.

Now that they had the hard drive, she was anxious to crosscheck the names. As she made it to the end of her memorized list of news sites, she let out a sigh of relief. A day without a reported death was a small but welcome respite from her daily anxiety.

But it hadn't been the only thing she'd been searching

for. With the extremist uprising in the prison camps, Mayhara feared for her parents and her sisters. She was sure her family, peaceful as they were, wouldn't get involved in extremist groups, but there was a constant dread that they'd get caught in the crossfire. Her fear that something might happen to her family had exemplified when she'd been marked as a fugitive. She was paranoid that the government would use her family as bait to get her to turn herself in. By some miracle, Darshana had used her connections to keep them safe—even if it was within the prison camp walls. Darshana hadn't been specific, but she apparently had undercover mages working as guards, and they had promised Darshana Mayhara's family would be kept out of harm's way.

She didn't know if she could count on that promise, but she had no choice but to accept it.

Again, she was relieved that her Linq search revealed no reported deaths. But that didn't mean the government wasn't hiding such news from the public. She did find a report of some of an extremist group's members being locked up in solitary confinement, but it wasn't from the camp her family were in. Mayhara shuddered to think what things must have been like in those camps. Her heart cinched at the thought of her family enduring any cruel treatment, but she had to count on Darshana's word that they'd be kept safe.

But she couldn't go on like this. Not knowing. She had to get them out of there. Somehow, there had to be a way.

"Yes," Darshana suddenly said. "That looks right."

Mayhara looked up from her Linq and stepped forward to glance at the monitor. Her eyes narrowed. "I've seen that before."

Darshana and Jae turned to face her.

"You have?" Jae asked. "Where?"

"CenSinq." Mayhara touched two fingers to her bottom lip as she stared at the scroll. "Where I used to work. It's in the director's office."

# Five

"Wait."

"Shiro, there's no time."

Shiro searched Qiang's face, not sure what he was looking for. Perhaps a sign that Qiang was not as brutal as he appeared to be.

"I'm just… I think we should think this through."

Qiang took Shiro's hands. His grip was strong. "I can sense your anxiousness, but we've talked about this at length. Shiro, this is our chance to get out of here. We won't get another one. We need to rebel. Now. We need to find the mages on the outside and come back and free our people."

Shiro swallowed hard, his throat like sandpaper. "I know. It's just… I don't see how violence is the answer."

"They're not giving us a lot of choices."

Shiro's eyes bore into Qiang's. "There's always a choice."

Qiang was locked into Shiro's gaze, as if his words were sinking in. He nodded. "I know. This here is a choice. What we're doing. We're choosing to free our people. This is a necessary evil for the greater good."

"I know, but—"

"And don't forget, Shiro: They were coming after you. If we hadn't left tonight, you might have been dead tomorrow."

*But we aren't out yet*, Shiro thought. There was no guarantee this escape attempt would even work. Reluctance kept Shiro from speaking, but as Peng and Bao called to them in whispers, he finally nodded once in agreement.

Qiang signaled for Shiro to follow him. They stuck to

the side of the dirt path, close to the tall grass. The orange glow that had burnt through the sky when they'd left their bunker had now faded completely to black. The twinkling stars above reminded Shiro of freedom, of home. Of lying beside the koi pond at the academy with the first boy he'd ever kissed.

A boy who'd been killed during the Eradication.

Shiro shook the thought from his head. That had been three years ago. And this was no time to get emotional; he had to concentrate on the task at hand.

The guard outpost came into view. The guard booth was a metal box pushed up against a thirty-foot-high titanium fence. Inside the booth were two uniformed men, and standing sentry in front of the gate was a uniformed woman. Two more guards were checking the engine of one of their jeeps parked about ten feet away from the booth.

Qiang gathered the gang into a huddle, the five of them crouched down in the grass and reeds. Qiang held a finger to his lips, and in that moment of silence, Shiro could hear the rushing water of the nearby river. The proximity of the water filled him with a sense of purpose. He could do this. They were going to escape. Tonight.

"Five guards are more than I anticipated," Qiang said, stroking his chin in thought. "We're going to need a distraction."

"I can cause a fire just outside the gate," Mitty suggested.

"Not a terrible idea." Qiang narrowed his eyes. "I'm just worried they'll linq headquarters, and then we'll have a whole mess of guards to deal with."

"What about a storm?" Shiro asked. "I can bring hard rain, and the emeralds can whip up the wind."

Peng and Bao smirked.

Qiang nodded. "That could work. No need to call it in; it's just a storm. Then we could get close enough to take them out and open the gate."

They all nodded in agreement.

"Don't forget," Qiang said, placing a hand on Shiro's arm, "this is just the inner barricade. Once we get past this, we'll need to book it to the outer one over the bridge before anyone finds out."

"Ready to make it rain, Shiro?" Peng asked, a sly smile playing on his lips as his palms began to glow a bright green.

"Let's do it." Shiro rubbed his hands together, his gaze

drifting toward the sky.

It started with small tufts of clouds appearing out of nowhere. The swirling gray grew thicker and expanded, stretching to block out the stars in a matter of seconds. It took every ounce of resilience for Shiro to withstand the piercing pain that sliced through his body. He squeezed his eyes shut, concentrating on pushing out his water energy and calling the element to do his bidding. His hair whipped to and fro haphazardly upon his head, the wind picking up thanks to Peng and Bao. The first drops fell lightly upon Shiro's face. And then it began to pour.

The rain was torrential, pelting his skin like small pebbles. Shiro could feel strands of his black and copper hair sticking to his forehead. He opened his eyes, but he could barely make out anything aside from Qiang through the curtains of rain. Leaves and debris zoomed through the air, twisting and turning and flying out of sight. The guards could be heard calling to each other to get out of the downpour, which kept violently switching directions due to the hard winds.

Shiro noticed Qiang say something into Mitty's ear, and Mitty nodded.

At Qiang's signal, they sprinted toward the guard

booth. The heavy rain concealed their footfalls. As they got closer, Shiro noticed the guards stiffen. He pushed out his energy to bring even harder rainfall, immediately feeling the sting of blood in his nose. Before he could calculate what the guards' next moves would be, a blazing fireball tore through the rain. It hit the guards' station with a blast, throwing fire in every direction.

Two of the guards were flailing, dropping to the ground and rolling to get the flames off them. The other two reached for their Comm devices. Shiro sent out a blast of ice to one of them, freezing his hand in place so he couldn't contact headquarters. Bao shot air energy toward the other, knocking him back hard against the wall of the guard booth.

Shiro felt the biting shock of electricity as he was suddenly struck from behind. He fell forward, the buzz of a guard's cyber baton thrumming in his ears. He looked up to see the guard hovering over him, drenched from the pouring rain, baring his teeth as he wielded the cyber baton. Before the guard could strike again, he was tackled from the side and taken down into a puddle.

The puddle seemed to deepen, practically burying the guard, as Qiang jumped off him and to his feet, his palms glowing red. He grabbed the guard's cyber baton and hurled it toward Peng. As soon as Peng caught it, he whipped the end horizontally, catching the female guard's throat. She clutched at her neck as she dropped to the ground.

Shiro looked around. Only one guard seemed to still be alive, but he was still on fire from Mitty's fireball. Shiro directed the rain onto the guard in hard torrents, putting out the flames.

Shiro locked eyes with Qiang as the guard moaned in pain. The guard's skin was blackened, his clothes burned away, and his cries of agony continued as he tried to claw at the ground and crawl away from the mages.

"He's suffering," Qiang said. "We need to put him out of his misery."

At first Shiro could only stare at Qiang, frustrated that it had come to this. His breaths were heavy, and his heart felt as if it had been shattered. Then he nodded and looked away.

The rain stopped, and there was a *thud*. Shiro didn't look to see what had been done or who had done it.

Shiro shook, his nerves on edge. Everything felt as if it had spiraled out of control. He almost flinched when

Qiang's hand stroked his cheek.

Qiang's voice was gentle. "We need to keep moving."

"No more deaths," Shiro said.

Qiang offered him a small smile. "I'll do my best. I promise."

Mitty, Peng, and Bao approached, and Qiang dropped his hand from Shiro's cheek.

"We've got about ten minutes to get to the next outpost," Qiang said. "Less if anyone saw that fire blast."

Qiang marched forward to the gate, his palms glowing red. His hands stretched out in the direction of the titanium posts holding the gate. The ground beneath the posts rumbled, the earth loosening into dust. The posts wavered, the thirty-foot gate leaning away from them. Peng and Bao threw out their air energy to push the gate farther, and Mitty charged toward the opening with his mighty strength, his arm like a battering ram, glowing with golden light.

With their combined efforts, the gate fell with a metallic *bang*. Dust flew about them in clouds.

The muscles in Shiro's neck and shoulders tightened as Qiang motioned for them to follow him.

They ran over the fallen gate together, following

wherever Qiang would lead. With the clouds of dust obstructing his view, Shiro relied on the sound of the river to help him get his bearings. He knew the bridge was downriver, and he could feel more than see which way they needed to go.

Just as they emerged from the clouds of dust, blinding white light beat down on them, stopping them in their tracks. Shiro's heart was in his throat, his hand pushing out and clutching for Qiang's arm. Someone shouted over a digital amplifier for them to stop at the same time that Qiang hollered for them to split up and get to the bridge. Before Shiro could protest, Qiang slipped out of his grasp and disappeared into the glaring light.

"Qiang!" Shiro yelled, suddenly feeling more alone than he'd ever felt in his life.

It took the sound of gunshots to knock Shiro out of his shock, his body crouching as low as he could manage as he darted toward the river. If he could get as close to the banks as possible and follow it down, he might make it to the bridge and meet up with Qiang. As his feet raced, so did his mind. He had no idea what he would do if he got separated from Qiang's crew. His breaths caught in his chest, and he could feel the adrenaline in his body pushing him faster.

Finally escaping the light, he caught sight of the river. The lights of the bridge were far off in the distance, but he wouldn't stop until he got there. He ignored the dryness in his throat from his rushed breathing and the sting of his racing heartbeat. He simply needed to get to the bridge.

Without warning, his shoulder flinched back. He stumbled, only understanding what had happened when the slick, warm sensation of blood oozed down his arm. At first, there was no pain. And then a tight pressure took over. He pressed a hand to his shoulder, gasping as the throb of the bullet wound worsened. He tried to get to his feet. His vision blurred. He could hear the guards approaching, the man on the digital amplifier instructing him not to move. And he could hear the river.

He couldn't let them get to him. The punishment for attempted escape was death. Not to mention, they already wanted him dead.

No, we wouldn't let them.

The pain in his chest and shoulder worsened. It made him wish he would just pass out so he wouldn't have to feel it anymore. But that wasn't an option. Not yet. Though he was losing blood fast—and consciousness along with it—he pushed out his copper energy and called to the river. He wasn't sure if the raging water was getting louder or if it was just the footfalls of the guards, but as he squinted, he could see the water surging.

He had to believe he had enough power in him to bend the water to his will. He had to trust that the water would take him away and somewhere safe. It would not harm him.

He rolled closer to the bank, despite the shrill command of the man over the amplifier. His head spun, and his body was soaked in blood, but still he rolled, the copper glow still strong enough to control the water.

There was a split second of freefalling, and then the muffled din in his ears as water enveloped him, nearly crushing him, and stole his breath. But in the next second he was traveling upon the surface, the rushing waves carrying him away from the gun shots.

He could barely see where he was. The lights of the bridge grew closer as his vision became clouded. The pain of using his powers combined with the gunshot wound intensified, feeling like ice in his veins, and Shiro cringed as he fought to keep in control. But it was too much, and he let go, praying the water would not betray him.

# Six

Jae made sure to follow closely. Although he'd pulled up the blueprints of the building back at the temple, Mayhara knew this building. There was no reason she shouldn't take the lead. They stood quietly across from the back entrance, waiting for the moment Mayhara had promised would come. Sure enough, just as Mayhara had predicted, the support staff entrance at the back of the building opened. A short woman in a cleaning smock exited the building but propped a broom in the doorway to keep it open before she made her way to the dumpsters in the rear parking lot. Mayhara had said the woman would do this, as she had every night for the past two years. She had either forgotten the lock pad code or lost her employee keycard or was simply too lazy to reenter the code whenever she took the trash out. It didn't matter to Jae what the reason was; he was just glad they had a way in.

Once the woman was out of sight, Mayhara gave Jae a nod. "Let's go."

It was as if Mayhara were gliding over the ground; her moves were smooth and stealthy. Jae kept close behind, emitting a bit of sapphire magic to keep their journey quiet. When they reached the door, they slipped inside. Just as Jae pulled his leg in through the doorway, his toe caught the broom. It swung downward, and he held his breath as he reached out and caught the handle. Mayhara looked back at him with wide eyes. He swallowed hard, hoping she could see the apology in his eyes. But the way she clenched her jaw seemed to be from fear of being caught rather than anger that he'd almost botched their break-in.

"This way," Mayhara whispered.

They followed the corridor, which was dimly lit by small yellow lights spread out along the hall. Before they reached the turn in the corridor, Mayhara stopped and held out a hand. Jae closed the distance between them, and she tiptoed to get her mouth near his ear.

"The first security camera is around the corner."

He nodded and stretched his neck, looking past her. After slipping his scrambler out of his pouch, he aimed the device in the direction of the camera. He turned a knob on the device until the small screen on the scrambler showed a dotted red line.

"Is it working?" Mayhara asked.

"Just retrieving the signal."

The red dots on the scrambler screen merged into a straight line. Jae pushed a lever, and the line distorted into peaks and valleys. Jae nodded his head. They both rushed around the corner and down the hall until Mayhara held up her hand again. Jae scrambled two more cameras before they reached the service elevator.

Adjusting his hoodie, he let out the smallest of breaths as Mayhara pushed the elevator call button. It opened right away, and they slipped inside. Mayhara pushed a button, and then she pushed back the strands of hair that had loosened from her bun. At first, they were both silent. Jae could almost hear his heartbeat. Mayhara looked up at him, and he searched her face.

"I was afraid for a moment the elevator's recognition software would identify me, but I guess they only have that software on the employee elevator." She shifted from one foot to the other. "Then again, I've probably been erased from the system."

"Unless they haven't done it yet, and you've set off a silent alarm. We can't be sure the system hasn't alerted someone that you're in the building."

"In which case the authorities would be notified, so we better hurry."

There was a small *ding* as the elevator doors opened.

"There's a camera directly outside these doors," Mayhara told him.

Cracking one of the doors open, Mayhara leaned away while Jae scrambled the camera's signal.

In the clear, Mayhara led Jae through the double doors, which opened up to a fancy corridor. The marble floors were polished, shining in the glow of the LED lights lining the baseboards. Mayhara sped down the hall and ducked into one of the offices, the door of which had been left open.

Jae nearly collided with her when she came to a sudden full stop. Her eyes were wide as she looked around, and she wiped at her jeans as if clearing them from sweat.

"What's the matter?" he asked.

"My stuff is gone. Not that it matters—it just threw me, that's all. I should have expected it."

She only cast him a momentary glance before she circled the desk and pressed a button on the computer. The screen came to life, and Jae waited patiently as Mayhara typed something on the keyboard.

Her face changed as she let out a sigh, and her shoulders dropped. "I'm in. They haven't changed the password."

He nodded, though she didn't see it. She was too busy typing away at the keyboard. After pulling out the portable drive Jae had given from her satchel, she swiftly connected the cable to the computer.

She swiped the back of her hand across her forehead. "It's transferring. It'll take a minute."

They locked eyes, with nothing to do but wait. The glow of the computer screen softened her features, the light thrown on her lashes creating impossible shadows.

She dropped her gaze, and he realized he'd been staring at her too intensely. He hadn't meant to make her uncomfortable. The situation was nerve-wracking enough without him gaping at her in fascination.

Clearing his throat, he turned toward the enormous window that looked out over the city. The lights from the buildings were like bright stars, and the colorful neon signs from the pubs and restaurants below added flavor to the darkness. He'd never seen any city from this height before, and he had a brief shortness of breath at the overwhelming beauty of it. As he placed his palm against the glass and scanned the city streets, he thought about how, looking at this view, one wouldn't be able to tell that the Eradication had even happened. No wonder these snobby office officials were oblivious, unable to see the impact of hundreds of families being arrested—even killed— because of the corrupt government and the Pishacha.

Before he could dwell on it further, Mayhara's voice stirred him from his thoughts.

"It's done." She quickly disconnected the cable and slipped the portable drive back into her satchel.

"Where to now?" he asked.

She pulled up the zipper of her jacket. "Top floor."

After switching off her monitor, she hurried out of the room toward the service elevator. With half their mission complete, Jae felt optimistic. They only needed to get the scroll and leave the building unnoticed. He held on to the vision of them succeeding, letting it drive him to finish the job. In the elevator, Mayhara pushed the button for the top floor. It didn't go unnoticed when she ran her hand over her satchel, feeling for the hard drive. It was as if she hadn't believed she had actually acquired what they needed. When she looked up at Jae, he gave her a nod, a silent reassurance that it was true.

The door dinged open, and they repeated their routine, scrambling the camera's signal before rushing through the double doors. This floor was even fancier than the last one, with elegant vases and expensive-looking artwork lining the hall. Jae followed Mayhara past a glass-walled conference room that was able to seat at least fifty people.

"There's another camera around the corner, and then the office is just down the hall."

With the camera signal successfully scrambled, they finally reached the secretary's station outside the director's office. Jae glanced at the gold nameplate on the door, which read: DIRECTOR SHEI.

Mayhara reached under the surface of the secretary's desk, searching for something. The corner of her mouth inched up, and Jae heard a click.

"Helps to be observant," she whispered before turning toward the director's door.

Mayhara went directly for the enormous mahogany desk. In her haste, she knocked over a framed picture that sat upon the desk's surface. As she straightened it, Jae noticed a beautiful woman in the picture, her chin up and her clothes impeccable. The director, he assumed. Beside her was a girl, probably a couple years younger than he was. Jae assumed it was the director's daughter, though the young girl didn't seem pleased to have her picture taken.

Mayhara crouched and reached for the handle of one of the drawers. Her face fell when it didn't open.

Ignoring Mayhara's muttered curse word, Jae crouched down to inspect the drawer. It didn't have a keyhole or lock pad, but as he ran his hand across the front, he found a small round sensor on the handle.

"It's fingerprint-activated," he said.

"Shit." Mayhara raked her fingers over her hair.

Jae scanned the desk. "Let me try something."

He reached into his pouch and pulled out a small leather container. Taking a small transparent sheet and a tissue from the container, he glanced at Mayhara to see her staring intensely at what he was doing.

"A little trick I learned a few years back," he said.

He carefully placed the transparent sheet on the side of the director's mouse and gently pushed with the tissue. Using the light of his Linq, he inspected the sheet. The lines of a thumbprint could be seen on the sheet. Jae then placed the sheet with the thumbprint on the sensor. A miniature green light on the drawer flashed as the drawer clicked open.

Mayhara's smile was wide.

He hesitated a split second, taking in the beauty of her curved lips, but then snapped back to attention and focused on the drawer as she pulled it open.

Mayhara pulled out the scroll tube, rotated the end, and then slid out the scroll.

Jae's eyes were first transfixed on the scroll tube. Though the room was dark and his Linq light too bright, it looked exactly like the 3D image he'd created on his laptop from Darshana's descriptions. His attention then went to the scroll Mayhara had unrolled. He noticed small dots of light illuminated on a map. Mayhara rolled it back up.

"That's it," he said.

"Yeah." Mayhara slipped the scroll back into the tube and slid it in her satchel. "Let's go."

Jae bent to close the drawer, but as he began to slide it closed, he heard something move in the drawer. "Wait a second."

He reached in and pulled out another scroll tube. It looked identical to the one they'd already taken.

Mayhara's brow furrowed. "What is it?"

"I don't know, but let's take it anyway. Just in case."

Mayhara took it from him and placed it in her satchel.

His heart was hammering through his chest as they made their way out of the office and down the corridor. They only had to escape the building undetected, and their job would be successful.

As they called for the service elevator, Jae could feel the sweat intensify on his brow. Every second it took to reach them felt like an eternity. At last, the elevator dinged. The doors opened, and Jae's jaw clenched. It wasn't empty.

A security guard flinched at the sight of them but was quick to draw his weapon. "Hold it right there!"

Simultaneously, Jae and Mayhara raised their palms. The hall lit up in blue and red. Mayhara threw out crimson energy, forming a crimson particle seal over the guard's hand and gun before he could pull the trigger. It hardened instantaneously. Eyes wide with shock, the guard struggled to loosen his hand from the crimson. Before the guard could use his free hand to use his radio to call for help, Jae bent at the knees and sent a kick into the guard's stomach. The guard was knocked backward and dropped to the ground. Jae reached forward and forcefully pulled the guard out of the elevator.

The guard somehow got to his feet and swiftly turned, swinging his arm and clobbering Jae's shoulder with the crimson-covered weapon. Jae howled in pain but immediately emitted sapphire energy to cause a high-pitched ringing in the guard's ears. The guard tried to cover his ears, but his one hand was still glued to his gun. Mayhara's garnet on her wristband glowed brightly, and then she expelled a blast of crimson energy to knock the guard off-balance. He stumbled backward, falling and hitting his head hard against the crimson stone around his gun, knocking him out.

"Come on!" Jae called, holding the elevator door open for her.

She ran to him, and he pulled her against him. He only let himself hiss through his teeth after the doors closed and the elevator descended.

Aside from their heavy breaths, they were silent for a moment.

"Are you all right?" she asked, her eyes on his shoulder.

He looked down to see his jacket had ripped. He ignored the throb in his shoulder. "Yeah, I think it's just a bruise. He didn't break the skin."

She nodded as she felt at the satchel, making sure everything was there.

Jae held his breath as the elevator doors opened at the service-level floor, but no one was there.

They raced for the door, and as they got to the entrance, Mayhara let out another curse. The broom was gone, and the door was closed.

Mayhara reached for the lock pad. After quickly punching in a code, the lock pad flashed red. She typed the code in again, but again the light flashed red.

"It must be a different code than I have," she said.

"Or they changed it when you got arrested. Here."

He swiped at his Linq and pushed on the screen a few times. As he held the camera of his Linq to the lock pad, a series of numbers ran across his screen. It stopped on a four-digit code, and the lock pad's light turned green.

The door had barely clicked open before they raced out through the darkness and bolted for his bike.

# Seven

Naree concentrated on keeping her hand steady as she fit the key in the lock. It felt like forever since she'd been to Jae's apartment, and a part of her hoped he might be home. Two Pishacha soldiers stood behind her, waiting to accompany her inside.

When she pushed the door open, she was not only greeted by a deafening silence and darkness, but memories of the time she spent in the apartment with her brother.

She'd come here for sanctuary after years of enduring her parents' insistence that she remain hidden. She'd grown up with no friends, no contact with anyone but her immediate family. She'd even been kept from meeting her grandparents, aunts, and uncles, just in case her secret would be revealed.

It was like prison, in a way. She'd spent her adolescence under the watchful eye of her parents, as they whispered and worried and cried about her safety. And when her brother had left for the mage academy, she was jealous. It was an entire school of mages dedicated to honoring her—her very own empire—yet she wasn't allowed to let anyone know she existed.

Finally, at sixteen, she couldn't take it anymore, and she ran away to find Jae.

She remembered Jae's intense discussion with their parents over his Linq as he tried to reassure them that he'd keep her safe, that she needed a little breathing room or else she might lose her mind. It took some heavy convincing, but he'd won in the end, and she was grateful.

One night when she was particularly sad, pondering her fate, Jae came to her and handed her a tiny, carved, jade dragonfly. He'd made it for her, explaining that dragonflies represented adaptability and self-realization. He'd told her that everything would work out, and she just needed to believe in herself, that he'd always be there for her.

Now, standing in his dark apartment, she longed to find the jade dragonfly. She needed a sense of meaning as well as the feeling that she could believe in herself.

"No one's here," one of the Pishacha soldiers said.

"The guard at CenSinq told the director the break-in occurred a couple hours ago," the other Pishacha said. "We need to search the place to see if they hid the scroll."

As the Pishacha began rummaging the apartment, Naree headed for the bedroom. Bending down and settling on her knees, she reached under the mattress, feeling for the place she'd hidden the dragonfly. The smooth feel of it made her smile. Quickly, before the shadow soldiers could see, she stuffed the memento into her trouser pocket.

Hiding her joy from having the gift in her possession again, she steeled herself and opened drawers and the closet doors. She doubted the scroll was here. Jae was smart enough not to stay at his apartment when Naree knew its location. He'd be somewhere she didn't know about. Somewhere secluded and concealed.

*My love, I long to see you.*

Kashmeru's words spread through her like warm silk. She wrapped her arms around her middle and closed her eyes. "I long to see you too," she replied.

*We're getting closer, but the necessary pieces are still missing.*

"I know. I'm doing what I can."

*We'll be together very soon, and then nothing else will matter.*

She nodded and opened her eyes.

The scroll wasn't here. What they really needed to do was get the other daggers. They were the more important elements.

She walked into the hall and called out to the Pishacha soldiers. "It's not here. We need to go."

The Pishacha stopped searching and marched toward her. With nods, they left through the door.

Naree cast one last glance at Jae's apartment before she turned to follow the Pishacha, the jade dragonfly cool in her pocket.

# Eight

Shiro felt the soft touch of Qiang's fingers interlacing with his. He stared at their joined hands for a moment before looking up into Qiang's shining eyes.

Qiang gave him a smile that sent a ripple of shivers up Shiro's spine, almost making him giggle. Qiang stretched his neck and looked toward the night sky.

"Look," Qiang said. "There's the comet."

Shiro didn't want to break away from his gaze. He could stare at Qiang's handsome face for ages. Reluctantly, he did as Qiang urged and turned his focus to the sky.

One could miss it if they didn't look closely enough, but Shiro spotted it. The hazy streak of white looked impossibly far away, yet somehow Shiro felt its energy. He remembered learning about it when he was at the mage academy. It didn't seem to be of importance, since the Lotus had not yet been reincarnated, but they were meant to study it anyway. It was supposed to mark the return of Kashmeru and the deity's hunt for his one true love, Lakshmi.

*Love.*

Shiro focused again on Qiang. He opened his mouth to speak, but all he could feel was pain. Qiang seemed to disappear as everything in Shiro's vision went black. Fingers slipped away, and an agonizing ache throbbed in his chest. He felt as if he were falling.

No. Not falling. Floating.

But he couldn't see where he was.

Shiro felt as if lead weights were pasted to his eyelids. He tried again to open them, confused by his blurry vision, and confused by where he was. The lumpy bed he lay upon was unfamiliar, and whatever room he was in smelled of moss and rotting wood.

He wasn't back in the prison camp with Qiang. That had been a memory. Something that had happened almost half a year ago. They'd run away. What had happened?

He lifted his hands to rub at his eyes but froze in place as his right shoulder seized in pain.

Agony.

*I was shot*, he remembered. *But not dead.*

The river must have carried him to a bank downstream, where he'd washed ashore. The only explanation for finding himself in his current location was that someone must have found him and brought him here—wherever *here* was.

He was thankful it hadn't been the Imperial Police. If it had been, he'd have been back in the prison camp. Or worse.

*Qiang.*

Though he could barely move, panic filled him. What had happened to Qiang and the others? Were they alive? Did they think him dead?

For a torturous moment, Shiro recalled the feeling of Qiang letting go of him. Perhaps he had had no choice.

Perhaps Qiang had been injured or shot and unwillingly let go of Shiro. They weren't supposed to be separated. They were supposed to escape together. Run off together. Start a new life, together.

Shiro attempted to move again. The spot where the bullet had hit him felt as if it were on fire, searing his flesh and ripping apart his nerves. He recalled a day in the academy when he walked too close to the golden mage practice area. A rogue fire ball had zipped out of control and smacked him in the gut, knocking him down. That burning ache had been the same. He'd eventually healed and gotten over the pain. He just had to believe he would survive this too.

Steadying his breathing, he listened. He heard water pouring. A rush of adrenaline coursed through him as he realized he was not alone. Using his uninjured left arm, he wiped his fingers over his lids and forced his eyes open. The blurriness slowly faded. Narrow streams of sunlight danced around the silhouette of a young woman. He found her to be the source of the water he heard, as she filled a clay cup on a cluttered table near the foot of the bed. She turned and left the room before he could get a good look at her.

He could only lift his head a fraction without pain shooting from his neck to his shoulder, so he glanced around the best he could from his position on the bed. He ran his fingertips along the rough sheets, and from what he could gather, it wasn't a real bed, but bound straw covered in blankets. This made him more aware of the room, which was constructed of thin planks of wood and bamboo, more straw and leaves fashioning the roof above him.

To his right was a small wooden table covered with flasks, glass vials, and a bunch of plants and herbs he didn't recognize. There was also a dingy mirror, cracked in a corner and covered with dust. He could see half of his face in it from his position. He almost gasped at the black, puffy eye staring back at him. The injury must have happened when he fell. His copper-streaked black hair stuck to his forehead from sweat, and his lips were cracked from being dry.

He glanced in the other direction. The doorway the young woman had left through led outside, and from what Shiro could see, the makeshift hut sat deep in a gloomy, overgrown forest. He could sense a murky water source nearby. A swamp, he believed.

The thought of water triggered a scratch in his throat. He needed to drink something. Eyeing the cup the young woman had filled, his fingers twitched. It hurt too much to move, but maybe using his powers would hurt less.

Bracing himself for the pain, Shiro raised his hand and stretched his fingers, his palm glowing orange as he concentrated on the cup of water. It began with a few drops hovering out of the cup, but those drops were soon followed by a steady stream of water that arched through the air toward him. Shiro opened his mouth and guided the water into it, instantly refreshed by the cool liquid. It wasn't until he took the last swallow of water that he realized the use of his powers hadn't caused any pain at all.

Instinctively, he reached for his neck. Instead of feeling the bulge of the power blocker beneath his skin, all he found were stitches.

"I removed it," came a crackly voice. "It will take some time to heal, but I can quicken the process."

Shiro half-expected to find the young woman from before. But in her place, there stood a boxy, elderly woman with scraggly, salt-and-pepper hair and sunken-in eyes. Layers of worn, beige material hung off her form in what Shiro supposed was a self-made dress.

Shiro's muscles tensed, not knowing what to expect of the woman. He looked her up and down, scrutinizing her, but she simply stood there staring at him.

"Who are you?" Shiro asked, his voice a bit raspy.

The old woman came closer with the help of a bamboo cane. "I'm the one who pulled you out of the river before you washed away."

"You pulled me out?" He hadn't meant for it to sound offensive, but he just couldn't picture a woman of her stature being able to drag someone from the river, even if he had been fully washed up on the banks.

"Maybe you're not aware," she said, "but mages aren't the only ones who possess magic."

Shiro looked her over, wishing he could sit up to inspect her more closely. "You're a witch."

"A swamp witch. Yes." She reached for a cloth that hung on a pole near the bed and proceeded to dab at the sweat on his forehead. "Though if I must be honest, my granddaughter did help me carry you here."

Her granddaughter. Shiro surmised it was the young woman who had poured his water. He looked past the doorway to see her sorting something into baskets outside. The girl looked to be his age, with clear, smooth skin, pale from what Shiro assumed was lack of sun. Her hair was a bit unkempt, the dark waves falling in a million different directions over her shoulders. In contrast to her grandmother's plain clothes, the girl wore a flowered skirt and a plain grey peasant top, so Shiro gathered that she must travel out into civilization now and then.

*Civilization.*

Shiro wondered how far away they were.

"What's your name?" he asked the swamp witch.

She gave him a slight bow. "Amalia. And that's my granddaughter, Karina."

"Not that I'm not grateful, Amalia, but why did you save me?"

Amalia pressed her lips together, her eyes narrowing. "It was an essential part of the prophecy."

Shiro almost scoffed. "Prophecy?"

"I realize you're not aware, copper mage, but the Lotus is in dire danger and needs your help."

This time he did scoff. "The Lotus? I think you've been hiding out in the swamp too long. There is no Lotus."

"On the contrary. She has been reborn. It's a well-kept secret—her reincarnation—but now the Pishacha have her, which means the empire must reunite and carry out its duty."

Shiro stared at her, unable to wrap his head around her words. "I… I don't believe you. What you're saying can't be true."

"Well, you best come to terms with it soon. Because it's the truth. If you search your soul, the mage in you should feel it in your bones. The prophesized comet is coming. The time has come, and the elite mages must assemble and fight, or it will be the end of us all."

# Nine

The sun had barely let go of the horizon when Mayhara opened her eyes. As her muscles awakened, she felt the residual ache of the night before. It wasn't from a fight or extreme physical exertion; most of their mission had consisted of sneaking and, at most, running. But she had been on edge so much, her muscles taut with tension and her body filled with anxiety, that the aftereffects left her sore and exhausted.

When they had arrived back at the temple, Darshana had been deep in meditation. Mayhara could barely keep her eyes open, so she had gone straight to bed, knowing they would deal with the scrolls and the external hard drive in the morning. Now that morning had come, Mayhara was filled with impatience, needing to know if they had all the pieces of the puzzle they needed to move on with their plans against the Pishacha.

She quickly dressed and headed down the spiral staircase. The morning sun cast a golden glow on the marble floors, and a cool breeze blew in from the veranda. Mayhara wrapped her shawl around her, breathing in the fresh scent of mountain air. She could use a coffee, but first she headed for the office.

She wasn't surprised to find Jae leaning back in the chair, scrolling with the computer mouse as he stared at the monitor. There were bags under his eyes, and his hair was disheveled.

"Have you been up all night?" she asked.

He straightened at the sight of her, rubbing at his lids as he spoke. "I got a couple hours of sleep. But I wanted to check on this."

She found herself staring at his biceps as he raised his arms over his head to stretch. Feeling a blush spread over her face, she averted her gaze.

The external hard drive was still connected to the computer, but the light on the device was off.

"Did the program work?" she asked.

"Finished collating at two in the morning." He crossed his arms as he yawned.

"Why didn't you wake me?"

"One of us had to get a decent night's rest." He gave her a half-smile. "In any case, I haven't looked through them yet. I thought you might be better at understanding it all."

"Let me see." As she made her way over to his side of the desk, she spotted a program running in the corner of the screen. She'd seen it many times before, so she wasn't surprised that it was there. Jae had found a way to hack into the city's facial recognition program the government used to keep watch for criminal activity. But Jae had been using it to track down his sister. "Anything on Naree yet?" she asked.

He stretched his arms again and linked his hands behind his head, letting out a sigh. "Nothing solid. I'm sure she's being clever about not being spotted—or she's using mage powers to keep the cameras from capturing her face."

"Or the Pishacha are keeping her out of sight."

"Though I'm pretty sure they're using her to get the daggers, and I can't seem to figure out which of the locations on Bruno's list of addresses is the next target."

"If only we'd still had Bruno's Linq, then we could cross-reference, or track down Naree by messages or email." She bit her lip, remembering that she'd accidentally crushed the Linq of the Pishacha soldier who Naree had been traveling with. Jae had the Linq on him when Mayhara had almost buried him in crimson rock, temporarily convinced by Naree that he was the enemy.

"Hey, stop blaming yourself for that." Jae leaned toward her and placed a hand on hers. "You saved my life."

The warmth of his hand was comforting, but she suddenly felt hot from his touch. She pulled her hand away and pointed at the scrolls on the desk. "Any luck with those?"

"The moving lights on the first scroll seem to match up with the uprising in the prison camps. I've been cross-referencing with some news reports I've found, so the director of CenSinq wasn't lying about those."

"And the black triangles?"

Seven dark grey triangular dots moved about on the map. At times, one or two of them would disappear from one location and reappear somewhere else. When Mayhara had first seen them, back when she'd worked for Director Shei, she'd asked her what they were, but the director had blown her off.

"I'm not sure yet. Could be the Imperial Police, undercover agents, or—"

"The Pishacha," Mayhara guessed.

Jae rubbed at his chin. "Can't rule that out, but I don't see why Director Shei would have access to their location. What purpose would it serve? Plus, I was under the assumption that there are more than just seven Pishacha soldiers—though I could be wrong. I don't think I've seen more than three in one place at a time so far. Our best course of action would be to check it out. Unfortunately, we don't have the manpower to cover all the spots they show up. And they keep disappearing."

"I don't think it's the elite mages. Otherwise, one of those dots would be sitting where the temple should be on the map. Could it be the location of the Sacred Keys?"

He shrugged. "I don't think so. There are still seven dark dots and we know for a fact one of the Keys is dead. I'd think either the dot would stop moving or wouldn't show up anymore."

Mayhara nodded, puzzled. "What about the other scroll?"

"That one has no lights or electronic signals of any kind." He took the scroll and unrolled it. "No tech. Old school. Another map, but I can't match it up to any land. It's not any of the major cities. I need to inspect it more."

"Has Darshana looked at them yet?"

"No. I've been planning on showing her once she comes out of her morning meditation. Come look at the collated report."

Jae slid his chair over, and Mayhara pulled up another chair from the corner of the room.

She looked over the window that popped up, examining the columns of information Jae's program had generated. It extrapolated the information from the academy's database and cross-referenced the census information, listing any known locations of mages residing in New United Asia.

Jae left the room for a bit as she looked over the files.

When he came back, he had two mugs of coffee. He handed one to her and sat back down. The aroma surrounded her, filling her with a sense of calm. She knew it was just a temporary feeling; they had a lot ahead of them. But at least she wasn't doing it all alone. She took a sip of the hot liquid and let it warm her inside.

"How's it look?" he asked.

"Looks like some of the files from the academy were corrupt." She shook her head as her eyes scanned names. "There's no way of telling how many of the elite mages were imprisoned and which ones made a deal with the government. But I see two that match up. The next golden and sapphire elite mages have addresses in the census database. They must have been recruited to work for the government like I was."

He sipped his coffee as he continued to gaze at the monitor. "They might be unaware that they are the elite if they haven't heard of the murders."

Mayhara nodded. "You're right. I'll get ready and see if I can track them down. The golden mage, Huojin Cho, seems to have the closest address. It's at least a start."

"And once you get her here, that will help with manpower too."

A voice from the doorway made them lift their heads. "That's assuming she comes back with you."

Darshana stood there, a frown on her face.

"Darshana," Mayhara said. "What's wrong?"

"I have some bad news." She stepped into the room and heaved a sigh. "The Pishacha have another dagger."

"What? How?"

"I don't know." Darshana rubbed one of her temples. "I just sensed a disturbance, and I know that's what it was."

Mayhara felt as if her breath had left her for a minute. Jae pulled out his Linq and began swiping and pressing on the screen.

"A death was reported in Gangapur City this morning." He reached for the scroll, unrolling it to inspect it. "There was a mark near there. It's moved now, but I remember seeing it because my family used to visit the Shastri Park gardens for my mother's birthday every year when we were kids."

Darshana pressed her hands together and placed them against her lips.

"Does that mean it's the dagger or the Pishacha?" Mayhara asked.

"I don't think it's the dagger." Jae shook his head. "That would be too easy, and if some of them are still locked up, it doesn't explain some of the dots moving around. But let me see if the location of the closest one is anywhere near an address on Bruno's list. I can go there and see what I can find out."

"Speaking of maps—" Mayhara picked up the other scroll and handed it to Darshana.

The guru looked it over, and her eyes narrowed.

"Do you recognize it?" Jae asked.

"No, this doesn't look familiar. I can't imagine what this place is."

"Do you think it's the scroll from your vision?" Mayhara asked.

Darshana ran her hand over the material. "It's important for sure. But I don't think it's the one I saw."

"But the container looked like these?" Jae asked.

"Yes. To the detail."

"That means it was made by the same scroll maker, right?" Mayhara looked them over, examining them for any differences between the two. "Here. The markings are numbers just along this line, almost impossible to see."

Darshana inspected the markings. "Yes, you're right."

"The scroll's design is unique, though," Mayhara said. "Obviously one that's been passed down through centuries within the company. I'd be willing to bet manufacturing scrolls was kept as a family business. Jae, think you can track down the scroll maker? I don't see a company name on it anywhere."

"I know someone who can help us figure it out," Jae said. "In the meantime, if you can get the vision of the scroll back into that brilliant head of yours, Darshana, and search for the marker number, I can use that. The company must have records of the scrolls it's made, and we might have a lead as to who has the scroll you envisioned or where it might be."

"All right. I'll do my best." Darshana adjusted the deep green scarf at her neck. "But first I need to go."

Mayhara blanched. "What? Where are you going?"

Darshana tucked loose white hair behind her ears. "I need to answer a call."

"A call? Who called you this early in the morning?" Mayhara asked.

"Not a call via Linq, silly girl."

"Oh." Mayhara fought back a blush. "Sure. Of course."

"I hope to return soon." Darshana's eyes darted between them. "Be careful."

She left without another word. Mayhara and Jae exchanged a glance, and then Mayhara stood.

"I'll start with the golden mage." She typed the address into her Linq. She'd have to take one of the cars in order to get there, but she was familiar with the route. "Wish me luck."

"Wait." Jae placed a gentle hand on her shoulder before she could get past him.

She faltered, almost turning into him just to feel him against her. She cleared her throat. "What's wrong?"

His eyes searched her face. "I'm just worried. There's been another murder. For all we know, there's been more."

She offered him a small smile, placing her hand on top of his. "I'll be careful. I promise."

"Keep your head covered and your face down. Lie low if you spot the police or anyone who might be Pishacha—"

"Jae, I know," she said, cutting him off. His concern warmed her heart, but she forced herself to remain practical.

"And only use your powers if absolutely necessary."

She reassured him with a nod. "Understood. You be careful too."

# Ten

Shiro scooped the last bit of hot soup Amalia had given him into his mouth, relishing the taste. She may have been a swamp witch, but she did make a rather tasty soup. He wasn't about to ruin his experience by asking her what was in it, however. He was just thankful he had one good arm he could use to feed himself. Being fed like an infant would have been humiliating.

Karina, Amalia's granddaughter, took the bowl from him. "Do you need anything else?"

"No. Thank you. You and your grandmother have been more than generous."

She offered him a smile and bowed before leaving the room.

Shiro desperately wanted to shift his position, but it hurt too much. Instead, he closed his eyes and listened to the sound of herons and warblers calling to each other in the surrounding woods. If he stayed perfectly still, he actually felt at peace.

But his heart ached, as if there was something missing. *Qiang.*

It occurred to him that this was the first time in years he'd been away from Qiang for this long. He'd been so used to seeing him on a daily basis, spending time with him, training with him, indulging in a few quiet moments alone with him.

Was it so easy for Qiang to let him go?

Shiro played the moment Qiang's hand released his over and over in his head. Was it intentional, or a means for survival? He told himself he was being paranoid, but the thought crossed his mind that Qiang might not have had Shiro's best interest at heart when he'd planned the prison camp escape. Did he even care about Shiro at all?

The sound of footfalls shuffling along the wooden planks of the makeshift floor roused him. For a moment, he tensed, wondering if he'd fallen into a trap. Maybe Amalia had contacted the authorities. Lied to him about wanting to help the Lotus. She'd be sure to get a hefty reward for turning him in, enough to get her out of the swamp and living decently. But then again, she'd removed his blocker, so that theory wouldn't have made sense.

He had to blink in disbelief when he saw his former guru from the academy approaching the bed.

"What? Darshana?" He attempted to sit up but hissed through his teeth when his shoulder throbbed, the pain pulsing around the bullet wound in his chest.

"Lie back, boy," Darshana said. "You nearly died."

Amalia, who had walked in behind Darshana, came closer to inspect his bandage. "This needs changing. I'll get more gauze and healing ointment."

Amalia stepped away, leaving Darshana and Shiro alone.

"She says ointment, but she means mud," Shiro said. "It smells of rotten eggs, but it does make my shoulder feel better."

"You should trust her," Darshana said, looking him over. "She knows what she's doing."

Shiro gazed at Darshana in wonder. "I wasn't sure you'd still be around."

"You shouldn't doubt me, boy."

"How did you find me?"

"Amalia."

He didn't question it, admitting to himself that he knew nothing about witch magic or their connection with mages.

"What are you doing here?" he asked. "It doesn't make any sense."

"Once you've had a chance to heal a bit more, you'll need to come with me. The mages are gathering. We have a lot of work to do."

He searched her face. "Amalia said the Lotus needs our help. I… I have to be honest. I have my doubts as to whether or not any of this is true."

"It is true," she said. "The empress has been reborn. Her name is Naree and she's been kept hidden away by her family, who have feared for her life since the day they found out she was the reincarnated Lotus. This is the hundredth reincarnation, which, according to the prophecy, determines the fate of the world."

"The hundredth time Lakshmi would deny Kashmeru her heart."

Darshana nodded. "Bringing about the destruction of the universe."

"But the empire sealed him in a tomb. The legend says he would unleash his Pishacha in an attempt to use the blood of the Lotus to set him free."

"The Pishacha are out there, Shiro. They have Naree—the reincarnation of Lakshmi—which means they're getting closer to freeing him from his tomb so he can carry out his destruction and the end of the world. The only chance we have to stop them is the union of the elite mages."

He was quiet for a while. He rubbed under his lip with his good hand, battling the sinking feeling in his stomach. A restlessness came over him, a need to know more. When he looked up at her, his expression was serious. "So this is it? This will determine the fate of the world?"

"Yes. And it is your duty to the empire of the lotus to stop Kashmeru from destroying it."

Amalia returned and placed a bowl of smelly mud on

the side table beside the bed. When she removed his bandage, Shiro held his breath. His eyes went to Darshana, who kept her expression neutral. It was only when Amalia slathered the salve on Shiro's shoulder and over his wound that Darshana wrinkled her nose. Shiro stifled a laugh, thankful for the comic relief.

Amalia cast a glance at Darshana, whose expression sobered.

Amalia gathered the old bandage and the tub of salve, ready to walk away, but Darshana's brow wrinkled. She grabbed Amalia's wrist, narrowing her eyes.

"What is it?" Darshana asked. "There's something you're not telling me."

Amalia took her time before she answered, her gaze moving between the other two. "You all know the prophecy. But there is a detail that has been lost throughout the centuries, one that is important to the one hundredth reincarnation."

Darshana raised her chin. Shiro wasn't sure if it was because she was insulted or simply curious.

"There are parts of the prophecy that remain in the ancient books." Amalia locked eyes with Darshana. "Parts that have been forgotten throughout the generations but are of utmost importance."

"Like the daggers," Darshana said.

"Yes. The daggers. But also the Council of the Seven."

Darshana narrowed her eyes. "I assumed that meant the Pishacha. It makes sense that the shadow army would be made up of his seven greatest warriors."

"I believe the translations may have been misinterpreted. I think there are pieces missing from the puzzle, and we might be mistaken about the Council of the Seven."

Shiro winced as he sat up a bit. "But none of that matters if we rescue the Lotus, right? If there's no Lotus blood, Kashmeru can't be set free."

"But do you think all it takes is the blood of the Lotus to open that tomb?" Amalia asked. "It's been sealed with witch's magic.

"So a witch is needed to undo the spell." Darshana wrung her hands. "One that is skilled enough to carry out undoing a powerful spell."

"Do the Pishacha have a witch working for them?" Shiro asked.

Amalia shook her head. "I do not know if they have one yet, but I doubt they will stop until they acquire one.

However, when they do, the witch would have to know *which* spell the original witch used in order to undo it. The spell was cast centuries ago."

"How would a witch know which spell it was?" he asked.

"A grimoire," Darshana whispered.

Shiro furrowed his brow. "Grimoire? What's that?"

"Every spell that's been cast has been journaled in a grimoire." Amalia paced, her gaze far away. "For something so important as sealing an evil god in a tomb, that spell most definitely would have been noted in a grimoire and kept in a sacred, hidden place."

"Do you know where it is?" Shiro asked.

Amalia dropped her gaze. "No. I don't. I'm afraid I can't help with that part of the prophecy, but I will try to find out. I've been shunned by many a coven, but perhaps I can find a kind soul who can forgive me for the wrongs I've committed."

Shiro almost asked her what she was talking about but thought better of it.

Darshana reached out and took her hands. "Thank you, Amalia. We'll need to find the grimoire before the Pishacha figure out they need it—if they haven't already."

They were quiet for a moment, contemplating their situation.

"So this is really happening?" Shiro asked, sitting up higher despite the pain.

Darshana released Amalia's hands and turned to him. "It is. But your help is needed." She stepped closer and sat on the bed beside him. "What is your answer, Shiro? Do you agree to fulfill your promise to the Lotus empire? Will you help us?"

He swallowed hard. It terrified him, but he knew there was only one answer. "Yes, Darshana, of course. I'll help."

# Eleven

Jae parked his bike off the street across from the gated house, making sure it was out of the view of anyone who would drive by. The house was a mansion, and Jae had to double-check the address to make sure he was at the right place. He still didn't know what he might have been walking into, but deep down in his gut he knew it had to be where one of the Keys lived. He just hadn't been expecting a mansion.

He jogged across the street, glad there was no one else in sight. If the black spots were Pishacha, he knew there was one not too far from here. He just hoped he had gotten to the house in time.

Glancing up at one of the gate columns, Jae spotted a camera overlooking the front entrance. The red light on the camera was on, and the lens was pointed right at him. He tightened his shoulders, his hands splaying and retracting. Fighting off his nervousness, he pushed the buzzer on the gate.

Moving his collar away from his neck, he ignored the churn of his stomach and waited. Though it must have only been mere seconds, it felt as if he'd already been standing there forever. He wondered if anyone was home—or if he was truly too late and the Pishacha had already found the place before he had.

The sound of a car engine reached his ears, and he glanced over his shoulder to see an approaching police car. He used his sapphire powers to listen to the inside of the police car. If the officer was calling in his presence, he'd have to abort his mission until it was clear. Jae ducked his head and pulled up the collar of his jacket, turning away from the street. He briefly wondered if the black spots on the map represented the Imperial Police working for the Pishacha. No sound came from the police vehicle, aside from the officer's breathing and the engine motor.

The police car passed without incident. Jae clenched his jaw and grit his teeth. He was in the clear for the moment, but he knew he still had a mission in front of him. Jae pushed the buzzer again.

"State your business," came a voice from the speaker box.

Jae knew he had to get right to the point. "I'm here in the name of the empire of the Lotus."

The silence that followed pushed in on his gut, harder every second. Still, he stood his ground, knowing the Sacred Keys' loyalty to the empress had to be strong. Otherwise, they wouldn't have been trusted with the daggers.

Unless he was wrong, and this address had nothing to do with one of the Keys. In which case, the owner could be calling the Imperial Police at that very moment.

Just as his doubts started to win over, the gate buzzed open.

The front walk was laid out in a curve, constructed in a mosaic of grey, white, and black stones, lined with perfectly manicured grass, vibrant flower beds, and water features. Jae cautiously made his way up the marble steps to the double-story, double-glass doors.

They opened automatically when he reached the veranda. Jae stepped inside, his eyes going immediately to the polished, white, baby grand piano that sat majestically in the center of the enormous foyer. A crystal chandelier hanging above it twinkled as it caught rays of sunlight. The house seemed more like a museum, everything modern and beautifully furnished. The Japanese, *ukiyo-e* print wallpaper featured gold birds and flowers, contrasting with the predominantly dark colors of the interior trim and detailing. The tall windows on either side of the main doors were paneled with colored glass panes of amber, green, and dark pink in a geometric design that represented leaves and cherry blossoms.

A burly man in a blazer entered from the right hall. Jae's muscles tightened at the sight of him. The man looked him up and down as he straightened the lapels of his dark blazer.

"Mr. Satoshi Kitaro is waiting for you in the formal dining room," the man said. "Please follow me."

Jae gave him a slight bow. The man turned, strutting

back down the hallway. Jae flexed his fingers before following him, hoping he wasn't walking into trouble. They walked through a small sitting room, where a fireplace was situated on the interior wall facing a floor-to-ceiling window. The tall mantel of birch wood flanked a rectangular mirror with gold-and-white-jeweled trim.

They continued through a center arch of decorative painted columns and molding with ornamental keystone designs, commencing into the formal dining room. At the oversized, dark wood dining table, in front of yet another fireplace, sat a man in an expensive suit, finishing his breakfast.

Jae studied Mr. Kitaro, still unsure if he'd just entered the house of a Sacred Key. The man's salt-and-pepper hair was slicked back, but a few stray strands had escaped the hair gel and hung to one side of his ear. His moustache and beard were trimmed neatly, and the ring on the man's left hand had to be worth more than Jae's motorcycle.

With no time to waste on being subtle, Jae emitted sapphire energy.

"Mr. Kitaro," Jae began. "Are you a Sacred Key?"

A soft blue glow radiated in the air: Jae's truth power.

"I am," Mr. Kitaro answered.

Jae's shoulders relaxed shortly. He wasn't in any immediate danger, but it was just a matter of time before the Pishacha found them both.

"Would you like to join me, Mr.—?" Mr. Kitaro motioned toward the table, his eyes full of skepticism.

"My name is Jae. And no, thank you. I'm here on important business."

"Yes. You mentioned that, Jae." Mr. Kitaro studied Jae's face and stance. He then turned to the man who'd led Jae to him. "It's all right, Aiguo. We're just going to have a little chat."

Aiguo nodded, but he didn't leave the room. Instead, he stepped back and folded his hands together in front of himself.

"The Pishacha are tracking you down," Jae said, disregarding Aiguo's presence. "The Lotus has been compromised, under the spell of Kashmeru, and the dagger needs to be moved before she finds it."

Mr. Kitaro regarded Jae, taking a sip of his juice out of a crystal glass.

Jae's hands itched from frustration. Why wasn't this man taking him seriously?

"I understand your concern," Mr. Kitaro said. "I am

aware that the Lotus has been reincarnated."

"Then you know that you're in danger. That the dagger needs to be relocated to a safer location. You should come with me. I can get you to a safe location."

"Safer than here? This house is a fortress. The dagger is in a safe. My bodyguard, Aiguo, has the strength of ten men. Why should I worry?"

"None of that matters." Jae leaned forward, his palms on the table. "The Lotus is under Kashmeru's spell, which means he can make her use her powers to get the dagger, and he can make her hurt you. You have a better chance coming with me, where the mages are gathering. They can protect you and the dagger."

Mr. Kitaro shifted in his chair. "How do you know I have no powers?"

"I'm guessing that since you're walking free and not in a prison camp, you serve no threat, meaning you have no powers. The Lotus and the Pishacha have already killed two Keys to get the daggers, and no one has caught them."

Jae waited a moment for Mr. Kitaro to process this information. The subtle clenching of his jaw told Jae that he hadn't been aware a second Key had been killed.

Jae pushed himself off the table. "There's a database

filled with addresses we believe they're using to find the Keys. That's how I found you, which means every minute you stay here, you're in danger."

"How did you get this information?"

"I have my ways. And I know you may not feel the threat yet, but we've obtained a digital scroll that might be tracking some of the Pishacha. They're closing in."

"What do you propose I do, Jae?" Kitaro asked. "That I simply abandon my home, my life, and live in fear as I anticipate the shadow army's appearance?"

The alarm suddenly went off in the house. It wasn't blaring, but loud enough to alert anyone in the house.

Jae recoiled and looked around, his body more tense than before. A video screen came to life near the doorway. Aiguo hurried to check the screen. Jae was right behind him. The monitor showed Naree standing by the front gate as two Pishacha used cyber batons to cut through the locks. They pushed the door open with force.

For a split second, Jae felt conflicted. Seeing his sister, he wanted to go to her, to rescue her from Kashmeru's hold and bring her to safety. To say he forgave her and promise her she'd be safe with him. But there was too much at risk. And there wasn't any time.

"Looks like you don't have a choice, Mr. Kitaro." Jae marched to the man's side. "We need to go. Where's the dagger?"

Jae could see the uncertainty in Mr. Kitaro's expression. The man stood, nearly knocking his juice over. He rubbed at the back of his neck and frowned. He clearly hadn't thought it would come to this so soon.

"I'll… I'll take you to the safe."

Aiguo followed them as they dashed down the hall to a locked office. Mr. Kitaro fumbled as he retrieved a set of keys from his pocket. It took him three tries to get the right key in the lock. Aiguo stood behind them, looking left and right down the hall, his hands balled into fists, ready to fight off anyone who might breach the safety of the house. When Mr. Kitaro finally got the door open, he raced to a painting on the wall. Swinging it away from the wall on its hinges, he typed in the code to the safe.

Glass broke somewhere in the house, and Jae's hands glowed blue, knowing the Pishacha had shattered the front doors.

"You have a back way out of here?" he asked.

Mr. Kitaro turned with the dagger case in his hands. "Yes. Follow me."

Mr. Kitaro grabbed a small briefcase out of the safe before closing it. As Jae raced behind, Mr. Kitaro led them to the far end of the hall to a descending stairway. They reached the bottom, and a chill seeped into Jae's bones.

All sound around him faded, a low whistle filling his ears. And then, his sister's voice.

*Jae, bring me the dagger.*

Jae shook his head, despite knowing Naree couldn't see him. She was using her sapphire sound powers to get inside his head.

They entered a room in the basement, filled with boxes and tools. Mr. Kitaro pushed aside a trick tool shelf on one wall, revealing a hidden corridor.

*I need the dagger, Jae.*

"No, Naree," he whispered.

*You can't stop destiny. This is meant to be. I will get the dagger one way or another. Don't cause me to hurt anyone just to make that happen.*

Aiguo urged them through the dark corridor.

"This leads to the back of my property," Mr. Kitaro said. "It comes out at the far end of the greenhouse. Aiguo can get us to the car and we can take off. Can you get us to your safehouse without them tailing us?"

"I'll do everything I can," Jae said.

Jae could just make out a door on the other end. When they reached it, Mr. Kitaro punched in a code, and the door clicked unlocked. He opened it and ascended the stone steps on the other side. He tripped as he reached the top and almost dropped the dagger case.

Jae caught it in his hands. "Let me take that."

Mr. Kitaro hesitated, locking eyes with Jae.

"Trust me. In the name of the empire."

Mr. Kitaro bit the inside of his cheek before finally nodding and releasing the case.

Aiguo made his way to the corner of the greenhouse and glanced around. "I think we're clear. Let's go."

Jae grit his teeth as he kept close to Aiguo and Mr. Kitaro, hoping beyond hope that Naree and Pishacha were still in the house searching for them. They rounded the corner, and Jae spotted the garage near the front of the house.

Suddenly, Aiguo was attacked from the side and smashed into the ground. One of the Pishacha had been searching the grounds, and it had paid off. Jae's palms glowed blue, and he emitted an energy wave. The wave blasted the Pishacha off Aiguo, but not without hitting the bodyguard as well. Aiguo rolled to the side with a moan but quickly jumped to his feet.

The Pishacha rose to his knee and stomped a foot down, extending his cyber baton so that the end glowed a greenish yellow. He got to his feet and swung at Aiguo. Jae created a vibrating blue sound shield and knocked the Pishacha back. The Pishacha swung the cyber baton, which cut through Jae's shield and caught him on the forearm. Jae hissed through his teeth, and his shield collapsed. He instead created a sapphire energy sphere and whipped it at the Pishacha. The Pishacha swung at the sphere with his baton but missed. Before he could counterattack, Aiguo jumped him from behind, his thick arm wrapped around the Pishacha's neck.

The Pishacha struggled, then dropped to his knees, still attempting to pry Aiguo's arm from his neck. His face began to turn blue, his eyes bulging from their sockets.

And then the space he was in burst into black smoke. Aiguo shuffled back a few steps, his jaw hanging open. The Pishacha had disappeared. Jae had seen it before, when he'd fought Bruno. Bruno had never resurfaced, as far as he knew, so Jae had to assume that meant the shadow soldier had been defeated, sent back to the depths of whatever evil place from whence he'd come.

Jae rushed over and helped Aiguo up, only momentarily regarding Mr. Kitaro's stunned stare.

"He's gone," Jae said. "But the others are near. We need to move."

*I can hear you. I'm coming for the dagger.*

"They know where we are," Jae said. "We've got to move now!"

Aiguo brushed himself off. "There's no way we can get to the car before they spot us. I have an idea."

Jae flinched at the sound of more glass crashing.

"I'll divert them," Aiguo said to Jae. "Make them think we're all in the car. Can you get him out of here?"

"Yes. I've got my motorcycle. He can message you when we're safe."

"We've got code words," Mr. Kitaro said. "I'll know if he's secure or in trouble."

"Good." Jae clapped Aiguo on the back. "Good luck."

Aiguo gave him a nod, then offered Mr. Kitaro a quick bow before bolting toward the garage.

Jae crouched down behind a bush near the greenhouse, pulling Mr. Kitaro close. They ducked their heads and waited as they heard the car engine start. The car peeled out of the garage, its tinted windows hiding who was inside, and left the property just as Naree and the other Pishacha raced outside.

"Let's go," Naree yelled, running off the property.

Jae kept still, praying that Naree wouldn't be able to hear him with her powers. The sapphire on his wristband glowed a bright blue, but he knew that even his extra boost of power might not be a match for what the Lotus could do. Another car's engine roared to life and took off. Jae kept a hand on Mr. Kitaro's arm until they were long gone. Only then did he dare emerge from their hiding spot to head to his bike.

# Twelve

Naree took slow breaths in and out, using her sapphire energy to drown out the sound of the Pishacha searching the Sacred Key's house. In her mind, a battle was taking place.

Hearing Jae's voice had done something to her heart. She missed him. He had always been there for her, yet now she was on the other side of the war lines. She reached into her pocket and ran her fingers along the jade dragonfly, holding back a whimper of frustration. What was she doing? If only she could speak with him, maybe she could clear her mind.

*My love, we need to stick to the course.*

Kashmeru's velvety voice caressed her, and her mind whirled. It was as if her heart did a complete turnaround. Kashmeru had an effect on her she could not control. She loved him. There was no denying what she felt. And when he called, she had no choice but to listen.

*Do you not want to be with me, Lakshmi?*

"Yes, of course."

*Why do I feel resistance?*

She didn't answer.

*Do you know what it feels like when I am without you? Let me show you.*

In the next moment, her heart felt as though it had been rammed into by a truck. Her breath left her, and her muscles tensed in agony. She doubled over, reaching out to grab something so she wouldn't fall to the ground. She gasped for air, clutching at her throat. As tears began to trail down her cheeks, she shook her head. She didn't want to feel like this. And it broke her heart that this was how Kashmeru felt without her.

At long last, the pain left her, and she was able to breathe again.

*It hurts me every second I am away from you, my love. I need you.*

"I don't want to cause you pain," she whispered, her voice rasp.

Please hurry, my love. Find the daggers. The comet nears. Its energy will help us complete the ritual, but we need all the necessary elements to make it happen.

She straightened, pushing her back against the wall as she wiped away her tears. "I'll do my best, Kashmeru. I promise."

# Thirteen

Mayhara adjusted her head scarf and pretended to be talking on her Linq, turning her face away from the Imperial Police car patrolling the neighborhood. She quickened her pace slightly, reaching the food festival that was taking place. It was safer here, crowded with patrons, and all cars were blocked from entering the festival area.

Glancing at her Linq, she checked her course and

continued toward the address she'd noted. There was an image in her head of Huojin from her academy days, but she wasn't sure she was remembering her correctly. The girl in her mind was petite but strong, with impossibly straight, black hair and an almost non-existent nose. She wasn't the elite back then, but she'd had that fiery spirit that could carry her there. The boy who had been the elite golden mage back then had been reported murdered a couple months ago, and this girl was the next golden mage on the list who hadn't yet been assassinated.

Making her way past a *takoyaki* stand, Mayhara ignored the rumble of her tummy. She probably should have eaten something before she'd left, but she'd been so determined to find Huojin that she'd left as soon as she could. Still, one whiff of the golden balls of fried batter filled with octopus, *tenkasu*, and pickled ginger almost had her doubling back to grab an order.

On a sign post she came to a hung WANTED poster with her picture on it. Murder, it read. A lump formed in her throat. New United Asia considered her a criminal. But she hadn't killed her friend. She'd been framed. Not that anyone would believe her. She pulled at the edges of her purple head scarf and kept going.

She had to push her way through a crowd clapping along to a Bollywood dance performance, getting annoyed when some spectators refused to move out of her way. When she finally escaped the throng of that crowd, she hurried past a few more food stands and an instructional yoga presentation for children.

A helicopter hovered past the fair, and instinct made Mayhara hunch her shoulders and duck her head. She peered up to check if it was an Imperial Police helicopter and then blew out a breath of relief when she saw that it was not. Her eyes already drawn upward, she caught a glimpse of the comet, it's hazy white streak a mere smudge in the sky. Its presence reminded her of her mission. She needed to find the golden mage and do it without getting caught.

When she reached a vendor selling *aonori* and *katsuobushi*, she paused to look over her shoulder. Someone caught her attention, someone whose stare was so intense, there could be no mistaking that she was watching her. Mayhara felt her heart pound harder as she turned toward the assortment of products at the vendor stand. Maybe she was being paranoid. Maybe the woman wasn't even looking at her. Mayhara waved off the vendor who was trying to get her to purchase his goods. She had to keep moving. Instead of looking back to see if the woman was still watching her, she squared her shoulders and marched farther down the lineup of food stands.

Steam from a *jalebi* cart surrounded her. She squinted as she made her way through, taking in the tantalizing scent of the sweet, deep-fried, sugary glazed dough. Again, she ignored the growl of her stomach, pushing through until she reached a parasol vendor. She stopped and subtly turned, finding that the woman was not far behind, and she was definitely watching her. Was she Pishacha? Or maybe undercover police? She was dressed in drab, grey clothes, a long, loose jacket hanging partially off her shoulders. Somehow Mayhara couldn't picture her being Pishacha or a member of the Imperial Police. So why was she following her?

Mayhara's senses became heightened, and her heart was racing. With tightened fists, she turned away from the street, cutting through the nearest alleyway, even though it would put her off course. She needed to lose the watchful woman first, and then she could double back once she was in the clear.

After slipping through the alleyway, she blended in

with shoulder-to-shoulder pedestrians. In a particularly crowded part of the street, she pulled her head scarf off her head and turned it inside out. The color was different on the other side, and it had a pattern, so she placed it back around her head with the light blue, flowered side showing in hopes to throw off anyone who might have been following her.

Making her way completely around the block, she found herself back at the *jalebi* stand. She waited there for a moment, checking all directions for the woman. She heaved a sigh and pressed her hands together to stop them from trembling, relieved that the woman was nowhere around. Pulling out her Linq, she checked the map again and continued toward Huojin's apartment.

The music from the festival faded as she got farther away from the festivities. Her Linq led her to an apartment building that looked to be going through renovations. Luckily, the workers had propped the door open to make their job easier. She walked past a man carrying cans of paint and headed straight for the stairway. The apartment number on the address she took note of told her Huojin lived on the third floor. She passed some people in costumes on the stairs, feeling a bit paranoid that she was the one being stared at.

Finally, she reached the door. She blew out a quick breath before knocking, then shifted from her heels to the balls of her feet as she waited. The door opened a couple inches, and dark eyes looked out at her. The eyes were bigger than Mayhara remembered. The young woman's hair fell in a curtain of silky black just shy of hitting her shoulders.

"Yeah?" the young woman asked, looking Mayhara up and down.

Mayhara cleared the dryness from her throat. "Huojin?"

The door opened a bit more, and Huojin narrowed her eyes, studying Mayhara's face. She could see the recognition dawning on her.

"You're from the academy," Huojin said.

"Yeah. Mayhara."

"Crimson house."

"That's right." Mayhara pushed the head scarf off her hair. "I need to speak to you."

"Why? What's going on?"

From inside the apartment, someone called out. "Huojin, who is it?"

As Huojin looked over her shoulder, the door opened more. Mayhara spotted a young woman with beautiful, dark skin and curly hair. Her heart jumped, realizing who it was. Meeting her gaze, the girl smiled, obviously recognizing Mayhara too.

Her smile widened as she got closer. "Mayhara?"

"Salina! Oh m—I thought you went back to Eritrea."

Salina ran up, immediately throwing her arms around her. She squeezed tightly and then took a step back to look at Mayhara. "I did. Back when my mom passed. I stayed to help my dad out for a few years. But, uh, Huojin needed my help, and my dad is settled now, so I came back. You should come in."

"Salina," Huojin mumbled.

"Stop worrying," Salina said, pulling Mayhara into the apartment. "We were close friends back in the day, remember?"

"You two were close friends. And you and I were close friends. But we"—Huojin gestured between herself and Mayhara—"never ran in the same circles."

"None of that matters now," Mayhara said. "The time has come for us to all band together."

"Why?" Salina asked. "What's going on?"

Mayhara looked between the two young women. "You might want to sit down."

Huojin gestured at the couch and chair in the small apartment. They sat, and Mayhara felt a churn in her stomach. This time it wasn't because of hunger, but because of what she needed to tell them.

Subtly, she glanced at their wrists. Each of them wore their golden mage wristbands, their citrine stones intact. It was a relief to see they both still wore them. Perhaps it was a sign that, somewhere deep inside, they were ready for what was coming.

She placed her hands together and stuck them between her knees. "I'm sure you've been watching the media about the Akutake comet."

"Yeah," Huojin narrowed her eyes. "What about it?"

"It's part of the prophecy. And I know this may come as a shock, but it's all coming true. The Lotus empress needs our help."

Huojin scoffed. "Lotus empress? Since when—?"

"They've kept her a secret for almost two decades. She's the hundredth reincarnation, which means Kashmeru has sent his shadow army after her. And they've got her. She's under his spell, and we not only have to try to break his spell and get her back, we need to stop the Pishacha from trying to carry out the ritual to wake Kashmeru from his tomb."

Huojin narrowed her eyes. "I don't know what street drug you're on, but—"

"I'm telling the truth." Mayhara fought to keep her voice calm. "You can ask Darshana."

"You know where Darshana is?" Salina asked.

"*She* found *me*, actually." Mayhara straightened in her seat and held her hand out toward Huojin. "And now I've been sent out to find you."

Huojin and Salina exchanged a glance.

"But doesn't she need the elite mages?" Huojin asked. "Excuse my crassness, but you weren't at the top of the class. It was Fei Ling."

Mayhara frowned. "She's been murdered."

"What?" Huojin's eyes were wide.

"No," Salina said softly, shaking her head.

"That makes me the elite." Mayhara waited as the information sunk in.

Huojin stared at her, her face falling more. "And if you're here to recruit me, that means that Kris… was killed too."

"I'm afraid so."

Huojin's lip quivered. Her head fell forward, and she began to sniffle.

Salina scooted closer and put an arm around her. "Oh my god."

Huojin wiped away her tears, lifting her chin a bit. "I used to like him. He was a great guy. He didn't deserve this."

"No one does," Mayhara said. "That's why we have to stop the Pishacha. They'll be coming after you next."

A wrinkle formed in Huojin's forehead. She blinked, then stood up. "No. No, they won't. I made a deal with the administration. They said I'm safe. I'll… I'll go to the Imperial Police and demand protection."

"They won't help you, Huojin." Mayhara looked up at her with pleading eyes. "They're in on it. The Pishacha are working with the government."

"No. I won't believe that." A sound escaped from Huojin's lips that was half-laugh and half-scoff. "They gave me this place. A job. They promised me my family's safety. I just need to work a few more years and then I can get them out. I let them put this damned blocker in my neck and vowed my allegiance to them."

"They won't follow through on their promises, Huojin. Believe me." Mayhara stood. "I was in the same position, and they came after me. They killed the wrong girl, and when they realized what they'd done, they tried to pin the murder on me. I'm surprised you haven't seen my face on the news."

Huojin crossed her arms over her chest. "I don't read the news. It's too depressing."

Mayhara folded her hands together and held them at her chest. "You have to come with me. Both of you. Darshana has a temple hidden somewhere they won't find. We're gathering the other mages and we're hunting down the Sacred Keys—the keepers of the daggers."

"Sacred Keys? Daggers?" Huojin shook her head. "What are you talking about?"

"I can explain everything when we get to the temple," Mayhara said.

Salina stood up, wiping her hands on her skirt. She appeared ready to go with her.

"No," Huojin said, her voice calm.

"What?" Mayhara could only stare at her.

"I'm not going." Huojin held her chin high.

"What do you mean you're not going?" Salina asked.

"It's the empress. We owe her our fealty."

"I can't." What might have been stubbornness in Huojin's expression changed to desperation. "They'll kill my family."

"They'll kill *you*," Mayhara said. "But if you come with me, we can beat the Pishacha, and we can set our families free."

Huojin's eyes filled with tears. "You can't guarantee that. You can't guarantee anything."

"I can only guarantee that if you stay here, they'll come after you." Mayhara slowly shook her head. "It wasn't that hard for me to find you, and I'm sure they're as resourceful as I am."

"Please," Salina said to her. "I came all this way to help my best friend. Don't let that be for nothing."

Huojin looked between them. "I… I don't know."

"Trust me," Mayhara said. "I was unsure too. But if the Pishacha succeeds, the universe will end. We can't let that happen. And the only way we can stop them is if we stick together."

Houjin's brows drew closer, and she fiddled with her wristband. Salina reached over and took her hands. Her eyes were on her, but she didn't say anything. It was almost as if they were communicating with their minds.

Huojin nodded, her shoulders dropping. "Okay. Okay, I'll come."

Mayhara felt as if she'd been holding her breath the entire time and was now able to breathe. "All right. But before we go, there's one thing we need to do."

"What's that?" Huojin asked.

Mayhara grimaced as she slipped a scalpel out of her satchel. "This is going to hurt a bit."

# Fourteen

Shiro slowly stretched his neck left and right, wincing at the slight pain as the movement pulled at his sore shoulder muscles. For the hundredth time, he thanked the gods that the bullet had missed his heart. He breathed in the faint smell of Amalia's mud salve, which was thankfully masked by the bandage taped to the wound on his chest.

He'd anticipated worse pain when he'd gotten dressed,

but it was tolerable. Whatever Amalia had put in the soup she'd given him was working its magic. He wished he didn't have to put on his prison clothes again, but he had no other choice. Amalia had nothing he could wear. At least the uniform was a plain color, nothing that would draw attention to himself out in public.

He froze in place, his fingers still on his shirt buttons. Out in public. It hit him hard that this would be the first time he'd see the city streets of New India in years.

Karina walked into the room, stirring him from his thoughts. "My grandmother packed some things for you."

"Some of that soup?" he asked.

"Yes, and more salve."

"Great." He held back a grimace. "Thanks."

Taking the sack she held out to him, Shiro bowed in gratitude and then headed for the doorway.

The humid air slapped him from every direction when he got outside. The hut sat in a dry, elevated clearing in the wetlands. Trees were all around, their roots buried in mud. At the nearest set of bamboo stalks, Darshana could be seen speaking in hushed tones to Amalia. Their expressions were grave. Darshana cast him a glance over her shoulder, and Amalia's brow furrowed with worry.

Darshana set a hand on Amalia's shoulder and nodded once before turning to approach Shiro.

Darshana took a deep breath in and adjusted the strap of her rucksack. "Are you ready to begin our journey?" she asked him.

He clutched the sack of supplies to his chest. "Yes, I'm ready."

They moved forward, off Amalia's land—if that was what it could be called—and into a mud-covered area littered with murky puddles, thin, bendy trees, and bamboo. Shiro scanned the landscape before them. The mud was held in place by old, dead leaves and stems of the plants that had probably died the winter before.

"Good thing I wasn't shot in the leg," he said.

Darshana regarded him with a simple "hmm" and continued walking.

Every step they took disturbed the mud, turning it dark and blackish as they tread, causing the scent of rotten eggs to waft up and invade their nostrils. Shiro could hardly keep track of their progress because of all the mosquitoes and other flying insects invading the space around his head and arms.

Farther into the wetland, the tall reeds began to tower

over their heads, with the fuzzy brown seed heads shedding their seeds into the wind. The humidity had Shiro's shirt soaked in sweat. To stop thinking about how much he wanted to change his clothes, he instead drew his attention to the jewel-bright, blue-and-red damselflies perching on the plants and the acrobatic tactics of the dragonflies hunting in the air.

"Darshana?" Shiro asked, cutting through the silence.

"What is on your mind, Shiro? I sense a lot of thoughts zipping around in that head of yours."

"What were you and Amalia whispering about when I came out of the hut?"

Darshana cast him a glance. "Please try not to step on the snails. We are the ones invading their territory, after all."

"Are you avoiding the question?"

"No."

Shiro swatted at a spider's web that hung suspended between two low-hanging branches. "I just... I just thought I should know. I'm about to do everything you ask of me, including sacrificing myself in the name of the empire, so if there's something I need to know, maybe you should tell me."

"We were discussing some points of the prophecy. It's been translated from the ancient language from centuries ago, and"—Darshana paused as she sidestepped a grass snake slithering near her feet—"we believe some of the points may have been misinterpreted—or left out altogether.

"Like the grimoire."

"Yes. And other things, perhaps."

"Such as?"

"We believe there is another factor included in the legend that has more or less been hidden from us. And I'm just now starting to put the pieces together. Of course, I can't be sure. It would be best to meditate on it. The gods will reveal the answers to me."

He didn't question her. He hadn't meditated since his academy days, and even then, he hadn't been very good at it.

After what felt like hours of trudging through the wetlands, Shiro noticed the trees beginning to spread out more. He felt a weight lift off his shoulders as they cleared the trees and were finally able to step on solid ground again. A sense of stability came over him, and for the first time in years, he didn't feel hopeless.

"You know, I used to think frogs were cute, but if I never see another one again, I'll be good with that. At least I still have my shoes. I almost lost them a couple times back there."

Darshana looked down at their feet, her brow raised. "You know, you could remove the water from the equation here."

Shiro gave her a sideways glance, and then his lips curled into a smirk. He could do what she said. It wouldn't hurt him to use his powers, he remembered. In fact, it would be rather thrilling. With his palms glowing orange, Shiro pulled the water out of the mud. Rivulets of water seeped away, leaving the hard dirt and grime to turn to dust and powder that crumbled off as they continued to walk.

"Much better," Darshana said as they reached an abandoned dirt road. "I'm parked just up here."

"Thank the gods. Don't get me wrong; it's a blessing to be able to roam freely without the threat of a guard's lashing, but that mud walk was a workout. I'll be happy to sit down for a bit."

"Speaking of being free, I have something for you."

When they reached the small blue car sitting halfway

in the grass, Darshana unlocked it and opened the trunk. Curiosity peaked, he stepped up beside her to see what she had for him. He almost laughed when she handed him a black windbreaker and dark grey baseball cap.

"A baseball cap?" he asked. "Really?"

She shrugged. "I passed a novelty shop on my way here. It'll do. Take it or leave it. But I'd take it if I were you. Word is bound to have gotten out that you've escaped. The authorities will be keeping an eye out for you."

He ran his fingers along the brim of the cap. She was right, and he knew it. He popped the cap onto his head and slipped into the windbreaker, making his way to the passenger side of the car. A strange feeling came over him as he buckled his seatbelt. It had been years since he'd had to do it. Though it was a trivial thing, it deepened his feeling of freedom.

"I also have this for you," Darshana said.

He looked at her hand to see she was holding out a wristband.

"Is that—that's not mine, is it?" he asked.

"It is now. Unfortunately your original one is stuck somewhere behind the prison camp walls. But I took it upon myself to have this one made for you. It might even be more powerful than your old one."

Shiro took the wristband and ran a finger along the surface of the carnelian stone. It was smooth and shiny, and the touch of it filled him with a sense of purpose.

"Thank you," he said.

"Well, you're going to need it. This is going to be a lot more than just a training exercise."

Without another word, Darshana started the car and drove them along the dirt road, flanked by trees on either side of them. Shiro thought the dirt road would eventually lead to a paved road or a rural street. Instead, it winded through a small village. The houses were small and in need of repairs, and Shiro even spotted a well where the residents of the village were fetching water. Though the people looked poor—their clothes worn with holes and their bare feet dirty—he felt their lifestyle was still a step up from his last few years at the prison. For one, they were free. And for another thing, they weren't being hunted by the Pishacha.

Shiro's chest felt tight. He realized that as long as he was a mark, he wasn't truly free. And if Kashmeru was successful in carrying out the end of the universe, freedom meant death.

"I guess I always wondered what I was going to do if I ever got out," he said, "but it looks like the only plan on the horizon is to fight the Pishacha."

"You learned this at the academy, Shiro. The mages have a duty to serve the empire, to do everything necessary to ensure the Lotus reigns and the world does not fall into the hands of evil. An elite's responsibility is even more important, as the head of their house, the role model and example to all mages, bestowed with supreme control of their power."

Shiro reflected on this for a moment, gazing out the window as they departed the small village. "But you're not just seeking out the elite, right? We should be gathering all the mages we can."

"I agree." Darshana nodded as she took a turn onto a more developed street. "And I do, in fact, have a mage who is not an elite under my charge. Strength in numbers rings true. Unfortunately, most of the mages are in prison camps, and my priority is to have the elite ready."

"How many do you have so far?"

Darshana worried her lip. "We have the crimson mage… and you."

Shiro's jaw dropped. "Two?"

"Mayhara is currently tracking down the golden mage. I have no doubt she will succeed in her mission. And we have intel on the possible location of the sapphire mage. That would mean we're nearly halfway there."

"That doesn't sound as impressive as you think it does."

Darshana glanced in the rearview mirror. "The prophecy states that the elite will be key to keeping Kashmeru at bay. I believe I am doing my part as quickly and efficiently as possible."

"All I'm saying is a little backup never hurt."

Darshana spared him a quick glance. "Is there someone in particular you have in mind?"

He thought about Qiang but shook his head. He didn't want to incriminate his friend if it wasn't necessary, especially after the brutal things Qiang had had to do. And the truth was, he was still hurting. Qiang had let go of him, had let them get separated. He had broken his promise to be by his side through it all. Part of him gave Qiang the benefit of the doubt that the blast of gunfire and desperation to stay alive had torn them apart, but another part of him wondered if it had all been a lie, if

Qiang had just been using him as manpower to help him escape, with no intention of being involved with him afterward.

Shiro felt the presence of water nearby. Sure enough, scanning the road ahead, he spotted a sign for the New Jaipur bridge. A sense of nostalgia came over him when he thought about the last time he had been in New Jaipur. He wondered how much it had changed.

The car shook, and Shiro wondered if they'd hit a pothole. He heard a horn honk loud and long, and the car shook again. Someone's tires squealed.

Darshana clenched her jaw as she held fast to the steering wheel.

"Is it an earthquake?" Shiro asked, his hand gripping the side of the car.

There were only two other cars visible on the bridge. The oncoming car swerved as the bridge trembled, crashing into the side railing. The car behind them stopped, switched on its hazard lights, and made a hasty U-turn.

Darshana stopped the car.

"What is it?" Shiro asked.

In the middle of the bridge, strutting toward them,

was a young man in a long, black trench coat. Behind him were three men who looked like ninjas.

"Are those Pishacha?" Shiro's voice was a whisper.

"I believe the three in the back are. Yes."

Darshana squinted. "I have a theory, but I thought it was just a myth."

"What's your theory?"

Before she could answer, the car wobbled. The man at the front of the group held his arms up, palms facing Darshana's car. Shiro let out a shout as the bridge rocked and the car was violently upheaved, flipping onto the driver's side. Darshana moaned in pain, her temple bleeding against the shattered glass from the driver's side window. Shiro quickly unbuckled his seatbelt, practically falling onto her. He got her free from her seat and mustered every bit of strength he had to lift her, despite the throbbing ache in his shoulder.

The Pishacha were fast approaching. Shiro used the dashboard and seats as footholds and hoisted the half-unconscious Darshana from the car. Her head was bent, and she moaned with every move. They both nearly fell as he maneuvered her over the side and got her onto the street. He then quickly carried her to the side of the bridge, breath labored and muscles screaming, his hands covered in her blood.

The mysterious young man at the front of the group raised his hands again. Shiro jumped to his feet and copied his stance, his palms glowing orange. Pulling energy from the river below him, Shiro shot out spheres of water, blasting hard into his adversaries. The Pishacha flinched back as they were hit, and then they ducked and moved, their bodies appearing as impossibly fast smoke and shadow.

The young man at the front stomped on the bridge, and it began to crack.

Shiro lost his balance, his shoulder aching as he caught himself from falling. He got to his feet and threw his water energy at the man, blasting it in an unrelenting stream. If he could keep the man from breathing air, he might get the advantage over him.

The Pishacha closed in, wielding cyber batons. Shiro backed up, ducking and dodging their swings, his adrenaline kicking up as he realized this could be the end. He hadn't come all this way to be killed on this bridge. Practically growling with frustration and panic, Shiro called upon his powers, pushing harder than he ever had before.

The bridge cracked some more, shaking and jerking, but below them, the water began to crash and rise. The usual gentle river became raging rapids, spraying up and pushing the bridge. Shiro focused and moved the water, pushing the waves toward his attackers. The water reached up like arms, the liquid fingers grabbing the Pishacha and flinging them downriver. They burst into black smoke before they could be submerged, disappearing into the wind.

One Pishacha remained. The mysterious man sneered at Shiro, his hands outstretched like claws as he came closer. Shiro thrust his palms forward. This time, he controlled the water in the man's body, lifting him from the ground. The man's eyes widened, his arms and legs flailing. Shiro clenched his teeth and flung the man back, hard, against the road. There was a crack as the man's head hit the ground.

He said something, something Shiro didn't understand, and in the next moment the last remaining Pishacha glided toward the man, lifting him into his arms, and the two of them disappeared into a cloud of black smoke.

Panting, Shiro stared in confusion. For a moment, he held steady, anticipating their reappearance. But after a minute without their return, he let his shoulders drop. The water below him dropped back to its normal level, the rushing slowing to its usual pace.

So this was what they were up against. He'd never imagined powers like what he'd just seen. They had learned nothing about Pishacha having the ability to evaporate into smoke. And the mysterious man—who was he? And what did he have to do with the prophecy? As he tried to wrap his head around it all, he heard Darshana moan.

Getting his wits about him, he darted for the guru. Dropping to his knees, he put his hands on her shoulders, looking her over.

"Are you all right?"

She lifted a hand to her head, retracting it immediately upon contact with her bleeding wound. "I can't tell. Dizzy."

He gently let go of her and looked toward their car. They couldn't stay on the bridge. The car's engine didn't appear to be affected by the flip, but there was no way to tell without testing it. Clenching and releasing his fists,

Shiro walked over to the top of the car and used all his remaining energy to push. After a few tries, the car fell back onto its tires. The driver's side door was busted and wouldn't open, so he went through the passenger's side and got into the driver's seat. He held his breath as he turned the key. Miraculously, it sputtered back to life, and Shiro released his breath. It worked now, but he didn't know if it would last long enough to get them somewhere safe.

Crawling out of the car, he rushed back over to Darshana. She hissed when he got her to her feet.

"You're losing a lot of blood," he said. "We need to get you help."

"We can't go to a hospital." Darshana grabbed him by the shirt. "They'll find us and end us both."

"How far away is the temple?"

"Still far. I don't know if the car will make it, especially up the hill we need to drive."

Shiro shook his head. "What do we do?"

She leaned against him, her lids heavy and her shoulders sagging. "I know of an abandoned supply warehouse near here. We'll go there and try to send for help."

# Fifteen

The top of the temple came into view as the car took the hidden path and rounded the final curve. Out of the corner of her eye, Mayhara caught Huojin's raised brows and widened eyes. Salina leaned forward from the back seat to get a better view.

"Whose place is this?" Huojin asked.

"Darshana hasn't exactly told us," Mayhara said as they pulled into the carport.

She put the car in park and paused for a second, noticing the other car wasn't there. Jae's motorcycle was parked in its spot, however, so relief washed over her at knowing he was back. Hopefully, his venture was as successful as hers had been.

She reached for the key to turn off the engine but stopped when the announcer on the radio mentioned the approaching comet.

*"...The New United Asia's National Space Association has sent a probe to gather pictures of the Akutake comet as it nears. It's still too far for civilians to pick up with ordinary telescopes, but NUANSA promises to upload any images they capture on their website. Scientists predict that the comet's intense energy waves may disrupt electrical equipment and devices when it gets closer..."*

Mayhara suspected it would do more than that. It was mentioned in the prophecy that the comet's appearance would be the pinnacle of events surrounding Kashmeru's reemergence. Its approach was like a time bomb, the closer it got, the less time the mages had to stop Kashmeru from destroying the world.

Mayhara grabbed her satchel and opened the trunk for the two golden mages. They had thrown some things together to bring with them, not knowing if or when they'd be able to return to their old lives. They couldn't take much, for risk they'd draw too much attention to anyone who might have seen them leave, so they'd had to restrict themselves to two duffle bags.

As Mayhara led them toward the entrance, a strange feeling came over her. She and Jae had only been working together for a few weeks, but she felt as if a bond had built between them during their time together. They were a team and they relied upon each other alone—aside from Darshana, whom she saw more as their leader. And even though she knew they needed all the elite mages in order to carry out their mission, the shift in dynamic made her inexplicably uneasy.

Once they were inside, Mayhara set her things down.

"You guys live here?" Huojin asked.

"It's temporary," Mayhara said. "I mean, I don't know what's going to happen after, you know, everything. But for now, it's where we hang our hats, I guess."

"It's so fancy," Salina whispered. "Like a museum."

"The main thing is it's safe." Mayhara led them into

the main room, which stood in the center of the temple.

Peering out the doorway of the office, Jae looked their way.

"Damn, who's the hottie?" Huojin's voice was a whisper, only loud enough for Salina and Mayhara to hear, but Mayhara had to wonder if Jae might have been able to hear her with his sapphire powers. She couldn't judge by his expression, which remained serious.

They approached each other, and Jae studied Mayhara, as if checking if everything were okay. She did the same, glad to see he didn't appear injured.

"Hey." Jae reached for her when they were close enough, but he then retracted his hand and shoved it in his pocket. "I see you've made some progress."

"You could say that."

"Did you have any problems?"

"No. I did think I was being followed. A woman seemed to be watching me as I travelled through the city's festival. Maybe I was being paranoid, but her eyes made me uneasy. I managed to lose her, though."

"Did she look familiar to you?" he asked.

She shook her head. "No. I don't think I've seen her before. And we were careful heading back to the car, so I don't think we were followed."

"Good," Jae said.

Mayhara gestured at the golden mages. "Jae, this is Huojin and Salina. Do you remember them from the academy?"

"Sure, hard to miss golden mages with your skills." Jae gave them a small bow, which they reciprocated. "Welcome to the temple. Sorry it's under such dire circumstances."

Huojin tilted her head. "I remember you now. You kept to yourself a lot." Mayhara tried not to notice how Huojin's eyes traveled up and down his body. "But I seem to recall you had some decent skills yourself. Are you the elite now?"

"No. No, we're still tracking down the rest of the elites, *including* the sapphire elite. I believe you're the golden elite now, Huojin."

Her expression changed, her flirtatious smile disappearing. "Yeah. It's still sinking in. The whole thing."

"Salina was staying with Huojin when I found her," Mayhara said.

"I've been away for a while," Salina explained. "I don't know if anyone remembers, but I left the academy when my mom passed away—this was months before the Eradication happened. Moved back home to Eritrea. But Huojin reached out to me recently, and I promised to come help her out. My father isn't in danger since Eritrea is out of New United Asia's jurisdiction, but Huojin's parents are in a prison camp, and the plan was I would pitch in whatever credits I could earn so she could afford to get them out once she was able to petition for their release. But I guess things have changed now."

"We'll get them out," Mayhara said, placing a comforting hand on Huojin's arm. "We'll get them all out."

Jae looked between them, eyeing their bags. "Why don't I show you the free rooms so you can put your stuff away? Darshana is out at the moment, but I know she'll be happy to see you."

"Sure." Huojin reached for the bandage at her neck, the remnants of where Mayhara had removed her blocker. She winced for a second, then turned to Salina. "You're so lucky you didn't have to endure getting a blocker or having it removed."

A man in a button-up shirt entered the room from the kitchen. He had a cup of coffee in his hand. Mayhara's brow furrowed and her eyes went questioningly to Jae.

"It's okay," Jae said. "This is Mr. Kitaro. He's a Sacred Key."

Mayhara's jaw dropped. "A Key? Does that mean you have one of the daggers?"

Mr. Kitaro extended a hand to Mayhara. "You must be Mayhara. Jae's told me about you."

A small smile found its way to her lips as she shook his hand. "I'm sorry. How rude of me. Yes, I'm Mayhara." When she released his hand, she offered him a bow. "I was just surprised at the expedience of Jae's success. Seems he tracked you down rather quickly."

"Well, it wasn't without its difficulties," Jae said. "I only got to him moments before Naree and a couple Pishacha did. Thanks to Mr. Kitaro's bodyguard, Aiguo, we managed to escape safely with the dagger."

Mayhara stared at Jae, worry washing through her as she checked him over, making sure he wasn't injured in any way. And seeing Naree had to have been difficult for him. She knew he wanted to rescue her. It was detrimental to their cause. But she wasn't here; he would have told her if she was. The frown on his face was enough to tell her that wasn't what had happened. She longed to comfort him. He caught her gaze, and her expression sobered. Internally, she told herself she was being overprotective and obsessive.

"Yes. Aiguo is a good man," Mr. Kitaro said. "I'm still waiting to hear from him to see if he got away."

"Pishacha," Salina remarked, shaking her head in disbelief. "That's crazy."

"I'm sorry." Mayhara pressed her fingers against her cheek, embarrassed by another rude blunder. "Mr. Kitaro, these are Huojin and Salina. Huojin is the golden elite."

They all exchanged bows.

"You are all rather young to have such an important task on your plates," he said, studying them.

"We were trained by the best," Jae said in defense.

"Yes, but your training was incomplete." Mr. Kitaro took a sip of his coffee. "You'll be up against entities that are centuries old. And a god with unparalleled powers."

"It can't mean nothing, though," Salina said. "Why would mages even exist if not to protect the Lotus, to ensure that the empire doesn't perish? We may be young, but I believe we've got destiny on our sides."

Mr. Kitaro appeared as if he were biting back a smile. "You make a good point. And for all our sakes, I hope you're right."

"Mr. Kitaro, I don't recall anything about Keys from the legend," Huojin said.

Mr. Kitaro took another sip of coffee and made his way to one of the couches. He took a seat, and Huojin and Salina sat on the couch across from him. Mayhara stood beside Jae behind them.

"Long ago, after the first reincarnation, the elders of the empire were concerned about Kashmeru's threats to destroy the universe. When the elders asked the prophet who'd announced the prophecy if there was any hope, he told them to look to the mages. Kashmeru had his army; the Lotus had to have hers as well."

"But where do the Sacred Keys come into play?" Mayhara asked.

"There is an order of the elders. They are the ones protecting the tradition, passing down the prophecy, doing what they can to ensure the empire doesn't fall. They were unable to stop the Eradication, but I think they knew it was coming to this, because they entrusted the Keys with the daggers."

"It was inevitable," Jae mumbled. "Unstoppable."

"But not without hope," Mr. Kitaro said. "The

daggers were a hidden part of the prophecy. When the elders learned of them, they took necessary precautions to disperse them and hide them, knowing they were the keys to bringing Kashmeru back to life. The Sacred Keys were given the duty of protecting the daggers."

"How are Sacred Keys chosen?" Mayhara asked. "Is it some kind of connection to the empire?"

"We have direct blood ties to the Lotus." Mr. Kitaro straightened his back as he said it, as if showing his pride. "Not the reincarnated one of today, but of reincarnations passed."

Huojin shook her head. "And what are these daggers for?"

"They are bound with a magic that connects to Lakshmi's soul, through her blood."

"Meaning… her spilled blood." Mayhara's voice almost broke when she said it.

"Yes." Mr. Kitaro stretched out his legs. "The seven daggers are needed in order to begin the ritual to bring Kashmeru back to life."

Jae rubbed at the back of his neck. Mayhara put a hand on his arm, wanting to calm him. No one felt easy thinking about the empress being stabbed, least of all her brother.

"Can I see it?" Huojin asked.

"The dagger?" The Key studied her. "It is hidden somewhere safe. And it's probably better if you don't know the location."

"The problem is we only currently have one." Jae cracked his knuckles. "The Pishacha have two of them. Not only do we have to recover them, we have to find the other four."

"*Seven* daggers?" Salina asked.

Mr. Kitaro nodded. "Seven mage houses. Seven chakras."

"Seven deadly sins," Huojin added.

"They are all connected," Mr. Kitaro said, lifting his coffee for another sip.

"Why didn't anyone tell us about the Lotus being reborn when we were at the academy?" Salina asked.

"Only a handful of people knew. My parents feared for my sister's life because of the prophecy."

Huojin tilted her head. "I didn't even know you had a sister."

Jae shoved his hands in his pockets. "My family kept her a secret. And I had to pretend I was an only child.

Darshana knew. Apparently, she had a vision and came to see my parents when Naree was born. I don't remember it because I was just a toddler at the time."

"Maybe they should have told us," Salina said. "Maybe we could have done something to stop the Eradication if we knew the one hundredth reincarnation had come to pass. We might have been prepared for some kind of attack."

"It doesn't matter now," Mr. Kitaro said. "We couldn't stop the Eradication, and now Lakshmi—Naree, now—is under the control of Kashmeru."

"What is he doing to her?" Huojin asked. "Besides tricking her into setting him free?"

"He's making her collect the daggers," Mayhara said. "Even if she has to kill to get them."

Jae compressed his lips and dropped his head. Mayhara felt terrible for saying it, but it was the truth. And the other mages had to know how far Kashmeru would go to make the prophecy come true.

"Do we have a lead on the other mages?" Salina asked.

"Yes," Mayhara said. "That's actually how I found you."

Jae's Linq let out a tone, and a wrinkle formed

between his brow. He studied the screen and gnashed his teeth. "It's Darshana."

Mayhara came closer, trying to catch a glimpse of his screen. "Something wrong?"

"I… I don't know. She sent a location Ping, but it disappeared."

"Because it would be dangerous if someone else were to see it," Mayhara guessed.

Mr. Kitaro stood. "She must be in trouble."

"We need to find her." Mayhara's blood grew hot, and she got a churning feeling in the pit of her stomach.

"Let's go then," Jae said, addressing the mages.

"Do we leave him here?" Salina asked, referring to Mr. Kitaro. "Should I stay?"

"The temple is safe," Jae said. "I don't know what kind of trouble Darshana is in, but we could use the manpower if it's the Pishacha."

Mr. Kitaro looked up from his Linq. "My bodyguard is on the way. I won't give him the exact location until he's sure he wasn't followed to the nearby gas station."

"Are you sure he hasn't been compromised?" Jae asked.

"We used our code word." Mr. Kitaro nodded. "It's

safe."

Mayhara clenched her hands into fists. "Let's hope you're right.

# Sixteen

Naree felt exhaustion wash over her. Bhutano insisted they travel to the next address on the list in an attempt to find another dagger, but their speculations were wrong. The house did not belong to a Sacred Key.

Naree had felt her energy drain as the Pishacha soldiers killed the family in the house, despite their innocence.

She wasn't sure she could do this anymore. The darkness in Kashmeru's core was destroying her. She was pure light, a goddess existing in goodness, yet Kashmeru's hold on her was too strong to resist. Whatever magic he had used to put her under his spell was tearing at the very fabric of her being. She could feel herself getting more lost every moment she spent under his hold.

*Time is running out, my love. This is no time to back down.*

"I'm just tired."

*Soon we will be together, and you can relax in my arms. We can spend a thousand moons doing nothing but holding each other, you enraptured in the blissful cocoon of my love.*

An energy came over her, as if Kashmeru himself was holding her. She almost moaned from the feeling of sheer exhilaration.

*Come to me, my love.*

"Yes."

*Find the daggers. We need them all.*

"I'll do as you say, Kashmeru. I promise. But the mages have one of them."

*Get it back for me.*

"I will."

*Do whatever is necessary to retrieve it from them. It's the only way.*

"I don't know where they are."

*Find them.*

She was about to protest that she didn't know how to do that when her Linq buzzed. She glanced at the screen and concentrated on the Ping location that flashed on. She quickly double tapped it to zoom in, memorizing the location on the map before it disappeared.

"I think I know where they are."

*Excellent. Get the dagger. Our fate depends on it.*

# Seventeen

hiro paced the concrete floor of the dark warehouse. It had been at least an hour since Darshana had used her phone to contact the mages she was working with. Since then, she'd been slipping in and out of consciousness. He'd put together some old boxes he'd found in the warehouse and covered them with a picnic blanket from Darshana's car. He didn't believe it was comfortable for her, but it was the best he could do.

The blanket was already soaked with blood. The warehouse's outdated first aid kit had provided him with a solitary strip of gauze and some medical tape, which he'd fastened to her wound as best he could. He checked constantly to make sure she was breathing. Other than that, all he could do was wait.

He wasn't sure whom to expect, but he hoped he'd recognize them when they arrived. She'd told him Mayhara's name, and he thought he had a pretty good picture of her in his head from memory, but that was from back during the academy days. She could look completely different now.

Darshana stirred, and Shiro ran to her side. Her eyes fluttered open halfway, and she opened her mouth as if to speak, but no sound came out. Her lips appeared dry, so Shiro held a hand over her face and formed a few drops of water, pulling from the humidity in the warehouse air. She licked her lips and swallowed, and then her eyes drifted closed again.

He watched her for another twenty minutes, afraid to look away. He'd wrung his hands so tightly, he could have sworn he broke a finger or two. His chest felt as if it were being compressed with a wire that was getting tighter every silent minute that passed.

What was he going to do if she didn't make it? What would happen to him if the other mages didn't find him? He had no idea where to go or how to find them. He'd be lost. A fugitive with nowhere to go. With no sanctuary.

A loud *clang* sounded from somewhere in the warehouse. Shiro jumped to his feet. Though he knew Darshana had sent for the other mages, the fact was that there were still Pishacha after them. His first instinct was to protect himself and Darshana. He readied his stance, palms up but not yet aglow. The sound of approaching footfalls grew louder. Shiro's nerves were on fire from the anticipation.

"Darshana?" someone called. The voice was female. Friendly.

Shiro dropped his arms and stood up straight. He took a chance. "Mayhara?"

First there was a pause, and then four figures came into the room.

At first, Mayhara's appearance threw him off, but as she came closer, he could see she was the same girl he'd remembered from the academy. Only more grown-up.

Behind her were other mages from the academy he couldn't recall the names of.

"Who are you?" Mayhara asked him. "And how do you know my name?"

"I'm Shiro. I'm the copper elite." He glanced back at Darshana, who was still unconscious. "Darshana found me and was bringing me to the temple, but we were ambushed. She's hurt."

Mayhara and the male mage rushed to Darshana's side.

"She's been in and out," Shiro said. "She's lost a lot of blood. I thought about slowing the bleeding by controlling the water in her blood, but it would be too risky. I could stop her heart if she's too weak."

"No, it's a good thing you didn't," the guy said. He stood and turned to Shiro as Mayhara held Darshana's hand. "I'm Jae. This is Huojin and Salina."

Shiro nodded, recalling their names now that Jae had said them.

"What happened?" Mayhara asked. "Was it the Pishacha?"

"Yes. And someone else."

"Was it the Lotus?" Jae asked.

"No. It was some man. Some creepy guy dressed in black with dark eyes. He was in front of the Pishacha, and he used powers to destroy the bridge we were on and flip our car."

Mayhara and Jae exchanged a confused glance.

"Who was it?" Mayhara asked.

"I don't know. But Darshana said she had a theory. Then they attacked us, and Darshana was injured. She never had the chance to explain her theory to me. I used my mage powers to defend us, and they disappeared."

"Let me guess," Jae said. "Into clouds of black smoke."

"Yes, exactly."

"You're in prison clothes," Huojin said. "Did Darshana get you out?"

Shiro shoved his hands in his pockets. "No. I escaped. Well, barely. Got shot and fell into the river. Luckily, I'm a copper and was able to make the water help me. Until I passed out, that is."

"How did you survive?" Mayhara asked.

"It's a long story."

Darshana let out a small moan, but her eyes were still shut.

"We've got to get her back to the temple," Jae said.

"We've got medical supplies there. I can stitch her wound."

"It's dark now," Salina said. "Will she be okay if she's moved?

"I think so." Jae was already lifting her, cradling her like a baby. "Let's get to the car."

They headed back the way they'd come in, their footsteps echoing throughout the warehouse.

"I hope you weren't followed," Shiro said, adrenaline rushing through him now that they were finally moving from their hiding place.

"So do I," Mayhara replied.

"We can't take her car," Shiro said. "It's barely running. I hope you've got room in yours."

Jae opened the door to the outside. A small car sat on the curb. "It'll be a tight squeeze, but we'll have to manage."

Salina opened one of the back doors, and Jae placed Darshana inside in a seating position. "Okay, just be careful. Sit on either side of her to keep her steady."

Shiro scanned their surroundings before he got in the car. Huojin squeezed in beside him, but she was petite, so it wasn't impossible. Salina moved Darshana's head onto her shoulder, not bothered by the blood. Darshana moaned, and her eyes fluttered open and closed.

"It's okay," Shiro whispered to her. "We're with the other mages now."

Jae started the car, and Mayhara glanced back at them from the passenger side. "You'll be okay, Darshana. We've got you."

They took off in the darkness, and Shiro didn't know what to expect.

"Do you guys have a plan for all of this?" he asked.

"We're still putting the pieces together," Jae explained. "We've acquired one of the daggers. In fact, we've got a Sacred Key at the temple."

"A Sacred Key?" Shiro tried to remember everything Darshana and Amalia had spoken about regarding the prophecy. He had to admit it wasn't all clear to him. "Is he alone?"

"He has a bodyguard." Jae glanced at him via the rearview mirror. "Though I'm not sure if he arrived safely."

Shiro was about to question him, but the car began to shake. The car jumped, and there was a commotion of alarm between them. Darshana fell from Salina's shoulder, almost collapsing onto Shiro's lap. He caught her and pulled her back.

*Not this again*, he thought, his arms shooting out to brace himself.

Jae skidded to a stop. Before them, the road was torn apart, pieces of earth jutting from the paved ground. Dust kicked up, hovering around them.

"Oh no," Mayhara said.

Shiro bent forward in the seat. Through the windshield, he spotted a beautiful young woman standing in front of them, glaring as her palms glowed a brilliant crimson.

# Eighteen

"It's Naree," Jae said, locking eyes with his sister. At the same time that he feared the look in her eyes, a sense of relief came over him that she was still alive, that no harm had come to her. Yet.

"How did she find us?" Mayhara asked.

"It might have been from when Darshana sent me her pinged location."

"What do we do?" Huojin asked.

"We get out of the car." Jae threw his door open.

"Leave Darshana here," Mayhara said to Shiro. "We shouldn't move her any more than needed."

Jae kept his eyes on his sister. As she came closer into view, he saw that Naree was flanked by four Pishacha and two other people dressed in black. They were partially hidden in shadow, but there was no mistaking the contempt in their expressions. The ones without mouth masks had matching tattoos on their necks, though Jae couldn't quite place the design. He didn't know who they were or why they were with his sister, but there were many pieces of this puzzle of a prophecy he hadn't quite grown to understand.

"That's the guy," Shiro said, coming up beside him. "The one from the bridge."

"And that's the woman I saw at the street fair." Mayhara grabbed Jae's arm. He could feel the panic in her touch. "She's one of them."

The one Shiro said was from the bridge glared at Jae, sneering as he lifted his chin. Goosebumps broke out all over Jae's skin, his brow slicking with sweat. He didn't know this enemy. He wasn't sure what to be prepared for.

"What are they?" Huojin asked.

"Some kind of dark soldiers," Shiro said.

The earth shook again, the ground around them cracking and rumbling. Naree's hands were completely covered in red glow; it was so intense, it reflected in her eyes.

The ground rose around them. Not just the mages, but around Naree, the Pishacha, and the dark soldiers. It was as if they had created some kind of arena, a cave-like place for them to battle. At first, Naree and the Pishacha and the others sunk into the depths of the darkness, but Naree's palms glowed red from using crimson powers, illuminating their location.

The mages huddled closer together.

"She's the Lotus?" Huojin asked.

"Yes," Jae said. "But, like I said, she's under a trance."

They watched from the cave entrance as Naree stood in the center of the space, glaring at them all. When her eyes went over Jae, he swallowed hard, wondering if the trance had disconnected her from him. Did she no longer see him as her brother? Had Kashmeru broken her emotions to the extent that she was willing to kill her own family?

Her gaze went past him and onto Shiro.

Jae's eyes narrowed. Naree's red glow morphed to white. The dark soldiers seemed to be laughing silently.

"Shiro," Naree said, her voice echoing in the raised earth around her.

"Why is she calling you by name?" Jae whispered.

Shiro shook his head. "I… I don't know."

"Shiro, I need you to bring me the dagger."

Jae looked over at Shiro. His face seemed pale, his jaw trembling.

"I don't have it," Shiro said, his voice unsure.

"But you can get it for me." Naree's feet barely seemed to touch the ground as she slowly walked forward, as if she were gliding instead. "I'm willing to make a trade for it."

Shiro visibly swallowed. "Trade?"

"Qiang for the dagger." She smiled at him. "What do you say?"

"Who's Qiang?" Huojin whispered.

"Must be someone you care about," Jae guessed. "Don't believe her. Look at her hands. She's using diamond mage powers to read your emotions. She's lying."

Shiro blinked, searching Jae's face. "Are you sure?"

Jae clenched his jaw. He pulled from his sapphire powers, trying to reach out with his truth powers to see if Naree was telling the truth, but she was blocking him. He couldn't read her; her power was too strong. Reluctantly, he shook his head.

"It's a simple trade, Shiro. Qiang for the dagger. And if you don't agree, then I have no use for him."

"We need to go in there," Shiro said. "We can't let her hurt him."

The mages exchanged looks, and then Mayhara nodded.

They followed Shiro in, Mayhara tight at Jae's side. Jae gestured for them to move carefully. There was no telling if the ground would give way. The cave walls concealed them on all sides, shutting out most of the light. The farther into the cave's darkness they got, the colder the chill that snaked over Jae's body.

Shiro glanced around. "Where is he?"

"He's not here, silly boy." Naree raised a brow. "But neither is the dagger I need."

Jae concealed himself partially behind Shiro so that Naree couldn't see his glowing blue palms.

"How do I know you won't hurt him after I get you

the dagger?" Shiro asked.

"I give you my word," she said, smiling her brilliant smile.

It was only for a second, but Jae's truth power broke through.

Naree's smile fell away. "If I did have him, he'd be dead."

She gasped, and then a sneer took over her face.

"She doesn't have him." Jae grunted as she pushed back on his energy, almost burning his hands.

The ground rumbled again. Naree's hands glowed red again. Jae could see Mayhara's hands also glowing red. She was trying to stabilize the earth.

"Where is the dagger?" Naree demanded to know.

Her hands switched to blue. She was trying to use truth to get them to confess. Jae mustered up enough sapphire energy to silence the mages. Even if they were to speak, Naree wouldn't be able to hear them.

"Fine," Naree screamed. "Have it your way. I'll get the truth out of one of you, even if I have to kill the others in the process."

She turned to the Pishacha and said something Jae didn't understand.

On her command, the Pishacha advanced, their bodies seemingly emitting black tufts of smoke as they marched. Jae's hands were already awash in a blue glow as the four Pishacha shot forward to attack them.

Jae and Mayhara took a defensive stance. The others followed suit, wristbands aglow. The golden mages thrust out their hands, and golden fire shot out at two of the Pishacha, knocking them back. A path of ice quickly snaked over the cave floor, knocking one of the Pishacha's legs out from under him. The other Pishacha stopped dead in his tracks, an earthy formation trapping his feet. He looked down and growled, then disappeared.

Naree's hands glowed emerald, her jaw clenched as she glared at them. A vicious wind ripped through the cave, throwing half of them to the ground. Mayhara grit her teeth, using crimson energy to keep her balance. She reached down and yanked Jae to his feet.

The Pishacha all popped out of vision, leaving black smoke, then reappeared in different locations, charging toward the mages. This time, the dark soldiers, who had been standing protectively beside Naree, crouched forward and held out their palms. No light glowed from them, but dark tendrils of black particles streamed through the air.

The sounds of crimson, copper, sapphire, and golden energy forces buzzed between them, colliding with the dark energy the mysterious soldiers on Naree's side were casting at them. The Pishacha pushed in, whipping out cyber batons and swinging them at the mages. Jae lost track of the others, focusing on the Pishacha in front of him. He barely had enough strength in his sound wave sphere to block the impact of the cyber baton.

Suddenly beside him, Mayhara jumped with a guttural roar and landed hard on the ground in a crouch, her hands aglow in red. The red glow traveled from her hands, over the cracks in the ground, and into the nearest two Pishacha. The one attacking Jae stumbled back but disappeared into a cloud of smoke before he fell. Jae was sure he would reappear again soon, though he didn't know when. The Pishacha only disappeared for good with a critical hit. If they wanted to be rid of them, they'd have to up their game. The other Pishacha clambered to his feet but got struck with a fireball that sent him spinning.

The Pishacha who had attacked Jae reappeared behind him, but the sound reached Jae before the Pishacha could execute his attack. Jae blasted the shadow demon with a resonating sapphire energy sphere, sending the Pishacha flying back hard into the cave wall. The Pishacha morphed into smoke. Jae's breaths were heavy as he glanced around. He hoped the hit was critical enough to have banished the Pishacha for good.

The dark soldiers were still on them, but the mages held their ground.

"They have powers. Are they mages?" Salina asked.

"I've never seen mages like those," Mayhara said. "They don't fall into any classification of the empire houses."

"Watch out!" Shiro yelled.

They dodged a blast of dark energy, breathing hard as they jumped back into a defensive stance. A mixture of crimson earth and golden fire energy merged together into a gush of lava, the burning embers forcing the dark soldiers back.

Naree let out a growl and held her hands in the air. Copper light glowed in her palms. Rain began to fall, putting out the lava fire. The dark soldiers smirked as they advanced.

Mayhara threw out her crimson energy and formed a barrier between them.

Shiro's palms grew orange. The rain that fell seemed to be pooling together in midair. It grew until it was as big as a wave, which then was propelled into the Pishacha and dark soldiers.

They sputtered as they tried to get air to breathe. The female soldier raised her palms and pushed the water away, crouching low to the ground as she advanced. She headed straight for Jae.

Jae sent a sapphire sphere once, twice, each time sending the female soldier back a few steps. On the third strike, he yelled as he pushed his energy out, adding an earsplitting ring to the sphere and making the soldier close her eyes and cover her ears, her head obviously full of the noise. Jae took advantage of the soldier's weakened state and pushed a final sapphire sphere at her, knocking her off her feet and back against the cave wall. Her head connected with a jagged piece of hard rock, causing her to fall to the ground, unconscious. A Pishacha appeared, wrapped his arms around her, and they both disappeared.

Naree's palms grew golden. A massive flood of golden fire scorched in a circle around them. The mages huddled together, flinching from the flames. Mayhara threw out crimson energy, causing the earth barrier to rise around them like a shield, while Shiro called upon his water powers to send a wave over the flames.

Naree sent fireballs into Mayhara's shield, knocking it down, piece by piece.

Huojin was exposed first.

"Don't even think about it, bitch!" Huojin yelled, heaving a fireball at Naree.

"Don't!" Jae yelled. "We can't kill her!"

Before the fireball reached her, Naree held her hands up, glowing green. Huojin's fireball ricocheted, zipping back toward Huojin. It hit her with an explosion, fire crackling over her body.

"Huojin!" Salina screamed, running to her side. "No! No, please!"

Huojin fell to her knees as the gold fire energy coursed over her body. Her limbs dropped to her sides, and her eyes glazed over.

Shiro shifted his focus and quickly expelled water energy, putting the fire out. Huojin let out a deafening scream as some of her scorched skin peeled away. Steam rose from her body as she threw her head back in agony.

Salina yelled in a rage, spinning fast toward Naree and raising a glowing, gold palm.

"No!" Jae yelled, pulling Salina's arms back. "She's the Lotus."

Salina screamed in frustration, the golden energy flying from her hands. But Jae had thrown off her aim. Salina's fireball hit the remaining dark soldier. He screamed in anguish, flailing until the flames went out. One of the last Pishacha swooped in behind him. He wrapped his arms around the dark soldier, enveloping him in his dark cloak before they disappeared into a cloud of black smoke.

Naree's face was red with rage. She breathed heavily, looking around as if to surveil her position. She was alone with one Pishacha. Surely, she would see that she was outnumbered.

"This isn't over," she said, her eyes boring into Jae.

The last remaining Pishacha drew near her. Purple energy wafted through the air, emanating from Naree's glowing palms.

The purple energy grew thicker, filling the cave in a dense fog. Jae couldn't see anything, blinded by the amethyst power. The fog seeped into his lungs. He began to cough, and he heard the others coughing too. They were choking on the fumes.

"Mayhara!" Jae called when he could catch his breath. The fog began to thin.

"Jae!" she answered.

"Mayhara." He waved at the air in front of him, catching a glimpse of her. "Are you okay?"

"I'm right here."

He reached out, and she found his hand with hers. He pulled her into him, wrapping his arms around her.

The purple fog thinned more, dissipating into nothing.

Jae looked around. Naree and the remaining Pishacha were gone.

Shiro and Salina were crouching next to Huojin, who was moaning in pain.

"She's hurt bad," Salina said, a sob in her throat. "These have got to be third-degree burns."

"We need to get her to a hospital," Shiro said.

"We can't." Jae clenched his jaw. "They'll find her and kill her. We need to get her and Darshana back to the temple. Darshana left me the number of an emergency contact in case we needed medical attention. It's the best we can do."

Salina helped Huojin to her feet and nodded. "Okay,

but let's hurry."

Shiro wrapped his hands around his neck and threw his head back. "Those dark soldiers. They were mages, weren't they?"

"They weren't Pishacha," Mayhara said. "They were like us. Except… filled with bad energy."

Jae looked her over. There was a cut on her temple. He placed a gentle finger on her cheek to examine it. "Are you okay?

"I think so." Her eyes were still darting around, as if paranoid the Pishacha would show up again. "You?"

He let out a deep breath and shook his head. "This is far from over. She won't stop until she gets the dagger."

"We need to find the others before she does—and somehow get the two she already acquired."

Jae rubbed a hand over his sweat-covered brow. His chest was tight, and his muscles felt like they were on fire. "Let's get back to the temple and recoup, figure out our next plan of action. We need to make sure the Sacred Key, the scroll, and the dagger are safe. First, we have to make sure Darshana survives."

"Yes," Mayhara said, her body aching from exhaustion. "We need her more than ever."

Jae studied her face, but Mayhara could tell his thoughts were on the mission.

"I have a feeling there's more to the prophecy than what she's told us," he said. "Let's hope we can put all the pieces together before it's too late."

The story continues in

**Golden Mage**

TURN THE PAGE
FOR A
PREVIEW OF
# GOLDEN MAGE,
BOOK THREE
IN THE
EMPIRE OF THE LOTUS
SERIES

# One

Salina pushed aside the gauze curtain and gazed out at the koi pond. The clouds had parted enough to allow some beams of sun to dance upon the water. She took a deep breath in through her nose and released it through rounded lips, attempting to clear her mind and ease her tensed muscles. She'd hardly slept, keeping vigil over Huojin as she lay wounded and suffering in her bed at the temple.

The newscaster on the televiewer caught her attention when he mentioned the Akutake comet. Turning away from the window, Salina tucked a golden-brown curl behind her ear and grabbed the controller, turning up the volume a bit. A petite woman with short, brunette hair tilted her head slightly at the camera. In the corner of the screen, a still image of the oncoming comet was displayed.

*"This is Akutake's second cycle through our solar system, the last one—182 years ago—bringing it roughly twelve million kilometers away from Earth. Astrophysicists at the New United Asian Space Agency predict the comet will come exceptionally closer this year, approximating the proximity to be a mere seven million kilometers from Earth. Its closest range will align with the air space above the city of New Delhi in India's district of New United Asia in less than a month.*

*"Though NUASA reassures us the comet does not impose a risk, a movement of the devout population across New India, between New Jaipur and New India, has encouraged citizens to offer greetings to Akutake in the form of prayers, meditation, and festivals honoring the comet. Because of this, the governor of New Jaipur has arranged a number of festivals to welcome the comet in its various phases of approach,*

*beginning with the Navratri Festival, taking place next week."*

A rustling of sheets made Salina turn. With a furrowed brow and a hiss through her teeth, Huojin stirred. Her dark hair was damp and clung to her temples. She wasn't able to move too much, with half her body covered in severe burns. Though Huojin would have been best treated at a hospital's burn center, it was too risky. Mages were outlawed, and walking into a medical facility, which would no doubt be occupied by Imperial Police, would mean certain imprisonment. Or worse.

Jae had acquired the help of a doctor who was willing to keep his mouth shut for compensation. The doctor had provided burn creams and ointments, dressing Huojin's wounds to the best of his ability with what little resources he could provide. Left with pain pills and instructions on how to change her bandages, the mages were on their own to help Huojin to heal. Only time would tell if it would be enough.

Luckily, Huojin's fire powers drew most of the heat from the burns, converting the element into vapers that were released into the air. The result was a very humid room.

Salina hurried to Huojin's side. Huojin's eyes opened a fraction of an inch, her gaze resting upon Salina.

"Sal—" Huojin's raspy voice was cut short by harsh coughing. She winced as the coughing fit jolted her body.

"Take it easy." Salina's voice was gentle as she reached for a washcloth on the side table. She dunked the washcloth in the small basin of water before gently dabbing at the sweat beaded on Huojin's forehead. It was one of the only places not burned by Naree's fire magic.

"Where… Where is everyone?" Huojin asked, her face still contorted from the pain. "What happened with Darshana? Is she okay?"

"Don't worry about that right now. You need to heal before you can deal with anything else."

"But is she alive?"

"Yes. But she hasn't woken up yet."

It had been a series of harried events since the battle with Naree and the Pishacha. Huojin's injuries had been the worst of them all, but Darshana had been hurt even before the battle had begun, and she had yet to awaken.

"I need some water," Huojin said, shifting slightly to sit up.

Salina poured her a glass from the pitcher on the side table. "Here."

"I can't remember everything," Huojin said as she took the glass. She winced as she sipped, and then she handed the glass back to Salina. "I remember the fire. I remember Naree and the Pishacha disappearing. And you bringing me to the car. But I must have passed out from the pain."

Salina released a shuddered breath, feeling the panic as if it were happening all over again. She pushed through the feeling and focused on the events that had followed. "We brought you here. Jae got a doctor to bandage you up."

"I think I remember that. It felt like a dream. A really… agonizing dream."

"He gave you a shot of morphine and left us some pills. But Shiro said he knows of a witch who could heal you better than any doctor could."

Huojin scoffed. "A witch?"

"Yeah." Salina gave her a half-shrug. "Unfortunately, he can't remember how to find her, and Mayhara thought it was too risky for him to wander off searching for her. He said we'd have to wait for Darshana to come to. If she ever does."

"Didn't the doctor help her?"

Salina stood and began pacing. "Yes, of course. He tended to her injury but couldn't do anything more. He couldn't be certain if she would remain unconscious or not without a scan. But since we can't take her to a hospital…"

"We can't do anything but wait." Huojin shifted again, drawing in a breath through her teeth.

"What do you need?" Salina rushed back to Huojin's side. "What can I do?"

"Maybe those pain meds?"

Salina didn't waste any time. She quickly uncapped the bottle of pills and slipped two capsules into Huojin's bandaged hand. Huojin slid them into her mouth and took the glass Salina offered her.

As Huojin leaned back against her pillow again, Salina felt a heavy weight on her heart. She hated seeing her best friend like this. Huojin had been her saving grace when Salina had arrived at the mage academy, taking her under her wing. She'd been there for her whenever she had needed someone, which Salina had often needed, being so far away from her own country. And she'd been her personal mentor during golden mage training, especially when Darshana had been too busy to advise her. She was her home away from home, the one who'd comforted her when her mother had died and had paid for her ticket home, and Salina would do anything for her.

To see her suffering like this was killing Salina.

"Are the pills helping any?"

Huojin squirmed, her face twisted in pain. "Not yet. I think I need a distraction. Talk to me about something."

"What should I talk about?" Salina steadied her breath, fighting off tears.

"Anything pleasant. Tell me about your home."

"Massawa was originally a small, seaside village. It extended over the same area as the Kingdom of Axum, which used to be called the Kingdom of Zuma. It has the oldest mosque in Africa—the Mosque of the Companions—which is believed to be the first mosque on the African continent."

"So it's old," Huojin said with the hint of a smirk on her lips.

Salina smiled, relishing in the fact that her friend still had her sense of humor. "Very old."

Huojin licked her lips and swallowed hard, her eyes

drifting halfway closed. "Tell me more."

"It is very hot in Massawa. There's not a lot of rain. Like, ever. It's famous for having very high summer humidity despite being a desert city. The desert heat and the high humidity together make it seem unbearably hot. But the sky is gorgeous. It's always clear and bright throughout the year."

"What about the food?" Huojin asked. "I bet the food is divine."

"I think it is." Salina laughed. "But my absolute favorite is anything with *hilbet*. It's like a paste made from lentils and fava beans. I remember coming home after grade school and my mother would already be preparing dinner. She'd make a stew called *tsebhi* and flatbread and *hilbet*. And I would always eat the most *hilbet*, which made my brother mad."

"Yeah, that sounds like you." Huojin smiled at her. "It sounds lovely. I wish I could visit there."

"You can one day. I promise. I'll take you there myself."

Huojin's smile widened. Her thin wisps of black lashes almost entirely blocked the view of her chestnut brown eyes. "Tell me more."

"Well, even though it's called the Red Sea, it is the bluest of blues you'd ever see." She let her head fall back as she recalled her youth. "I remember going to the shore with my family when no one had to work or go to school. Those were the best days. They were precious to us. We didn't have a lot of money, but we felt rich because of the love our family had for each other."

When Salina looked back at Huojin, her eyes were closed, and a small smile rested on her lips. Her slow, steady breathing told Salina she'd fallen asleep.

Salina stood, her heart feeling compressed with worry. It wasn't so long ago that she had lost her mother. She wouldn't be able to bear it if she lost her best friend too.

READ MORE OF GOLDEN MAGE

AVAILABLE NOW

From Snowy Wings Publishing

http://books2read.com/GoldenMage

In case you missed it…

Be sure to check out book one in the

Empire of the Lotus series:


## CRIMSON MAGE


Available from all online retailers

http://books2read.com/crimsonmage

# ACKNOWLEDGEMENTS

I write to entertain, and it touches my heart when others partake in what I have to offer. I have a great writing community to thank for keeping me motivated, as well as friends and family who cheer me on, and to them I am always grateful.

Thanks to those who continue to support me: my best friends back home, especially Bonnie, Sasha, Carol, and Rose. Thanks to my colleagues, and of course my family.

High fives to my ARC team—especially Kalli Bunch, for all their awesome feedback and encouragement.

I hope everyone sticks around for the rest of the series, and I hope I can live up to your expectations.

And thank you, Kirsten, for another awesome cover!

# ABOUT THE AUTHOR

Dorothy Dreyer is a Philippine-born American living in Germany with her husband, her two college kids, and two Siberian Huskies. She is an award-winning, *USA Today* Bestselling Author of young adult and new adult books that usually have some element of magic or the supernatural in them. Aside from reading, she enjoys movies, binge-watching series, chocolate, take-out, traveling, and having fun with friends and family.

You can find out more about Dorothy on her website: http://dorothydreyer.com

## ALSO FROM
## SNOWY WINGS PUBLISHING

### WHEN DARKNESS WHISPERS

by Heather L. Reid

### KILL ME ONCE, KILL ME TWICE

by Clara Kensie

### ALL THE TALES WE TELL

by Annie Cosby

Find them and more at

https://www.snowywingspublishing.com/books

www.ingramcontent.com/pod-product-compliance
Lightning Source LLC
Chambersburg PA
CBHW050522190726

48284CB00003B/906